Leaving Gee's Bend

Leaving Gee's Bend

IRENE LATHAM

G. P. PUTNAM'S SONS
AN IMPRINT OF PENGUIN GROUP (USA) INC.

G. P. PUTNAM'S SONS
A division of Penguin Young Readers Group.
Published by The Penguin Group.
Penguin Group (USA) Inc. , 375 Hudson Street, New York, NY 10014, U.S.A.
Penguin Group (Canada), 90 Eglinton Avenue East, Suite 700, Toronto,
Ontario M4P 2Y3, Canada (a division of Pearson Penguin Canada Inc.).
Penguin Books Ltd, 80 Strand, London WC2R 0RL, England.
Penguin Ireland, 25 St. Stephen's Green, Dublin 2, Ireland (a division of Penguin Books Ltd.).
Penguin Group (Australia), 250 Camberwell Road, Camberwell, Victoria 3124, Australia
(a division of Pearson Australia Group Pty Ltd).
Penguin Books India Pvt Ltd, 11 Community Centre, Panchsheel Park,
New Delhi—110 017, India.
Penguin Group (NZ), 67 Apollo Drive, Rosedale, North Shore 0632, New Zealand
(a division of Pearson New Zealand Ltd).
Penguin Books (South Africa) (Pty) Ltd, 24 Sturdee Avenue, Rosebank,
Johannesburg 2196, South Africa.
Penguin Books Ltd, Registered Offices: 80 Strand, London WC2R 0RL, England.

Design by Katrina Damkoehler. Text set in Cochin Medium.

Library of Congress Cataloging-in-Publication Data
Latham, Irene.
Leaving Gee's Bend / Irene Latham. p. cm.
Summary: Ludelphia Bennett, a determined, ten-year-old African American girl in
1932 Gee's Bend, Alabama, leaves home in an effort to find medical help for her sick mother,
and she recounts her ensuing adventures in a quilt she is making.
[1. Quilting—Fiction. 2. Quilts—Fiction. 3. African Americans—Fiction.
4. Alabama—History—1819–1950—Fiction.] I. Title.
PZ7.L3476Le 2010 [Fic]—dc22 2009008732

ISBN 978-0-399-25179-5
1 3 5 7 9 10 8 6 4 2

in memory of

Bobbie Nell Holcomb Latham
who loved quilts

and

Allie Ludelphia Threadgill Holcomb
who created them

Contents

One Eye That Works

MAMA PULLED A CHICKEN EGG FROM BEHIND THE azalea bush in our front yard and narrowed her eyes. "Ludelphia Bennett! You go back in there and get your eye patch."

I jumped off the edge of the porch. Mama always noticed right away when that old triangle of denim wasn't strapped to my right eye. Didn't matter that she hadn't hardly slept a wink on account of the awful cough that seemed to come from someplace deep inside her. She knew my eye was bare.

I walked two steps toward the woodpile. "I'm only going out to feed Delilah." Now that I was closer to Mama, I could see her cheeks was missing the brown glow that always reminded me of the smooth bottom of an acorn. The brown glow that made us look so much alike. Instead her whole face had a tired gray look to it, and her long, thin fingers shook as she slid the egg into the deep pockets of her apron.

Mama moved on to the next bush without giving me another glance. "Don't matter," she said. "Ain't polite to be showing that eye."

"But, Mama!" I stomped my feet in the dirt. I didn't like that old eye patch. It itched so bad sometimes I couldn't think of nothing else.

Besides, Delilah was waiting for her breakfast. She stood at the corner of the barn same as she did every morning, her big ears standing up tall and her eyes bright, not doing nothing at all except waiting for me to get past the woodpile so she could start braying to the whole wide world that she was about to get her belly full.

Daddy said he ain't never seen a mule disagreeable as Delilah. Seemed like if the sun was shining too bright she'd up and decide not to work. But me and Delilah, we got on just fine—I reckon because Delilah never once complained about whether or not I was wearing my eye patch.

Suddenly a fit of coughing took hold of Mama's body. She bent over and grabbed on to her knees till it passed. As she straightened herself up, she wiped her mouth with the back of her hand, then reached around and pressed the palm against her hip. A sharp breeze caught the tail of her apron and made it fly up like a kite. Beneath the apron, Mama's belly bulged with baby.

"Delilah can wait just a minute," Mama said, her voice coming out jagged as a saw blade. "She won't starve in the time it takes you to go back in there and get your eye patch."

I crossed my arms against my chest. Ain't my fault I only got one eye that works. Just because the other one's stuck in my head like an old marble that nobody can play with. Ain't no need to cover it up, like the whole thing never did happen. Folks in Gee's Bend got better things to think about than what's polite and what ain't. Like them fields. Don't matter what season it is, there's always picking or planting or pulling to be done.

I mean to tell you, there ain't noplace in the world like Gee's Bend. For one thing, you can't hardly find it. It's like a little island sitting just about in the middle of the state of Alabama. Only instead of ocean water, it's caught up on three sides by a curve in the Alabama River. Ain't noplace in Gee's Bend you can't get to by setting one foot after another into that orange dirt that likes to settle right between your toes. I reckon the hard part is how once you're in Gee's Bend, it ain't all that easy to get out.

But that didn't matter much to me, not on that November morning in 1932 when I was just ten years old.

And wasn't no point in arguing with Mama, neither. She'd take a switch to me if I sassed her. Didn't make no difference that she had a baby on the way and a barking cough that was keeping her up nights. Wasn't much of nothing that would keep her from doing all the chores a mama's got to do.

I turned back to the cabin and climbed the steps two at a time. I knew I'd best get on back in there and get my eye patch from under the pillow. But I stopped on the top step when I saw the way Mama hunched over the last azalea bush, the baby in her belly pulling her whole body low to the ground. Three times in my life I'd seen her look like this. But them babies didn't make it, on account they was born too soon.

What if this one didn't make it neither?

Mama always got real quiet after Daddy shoveled the last bit of dirt over the grave and Reverend Irvin stuck in one of them little white crosses. Last time that quiet lasted from planting time to harvest.

I slipped my fingers into the front pocket of my sack dress and felt for the needle and scraps of cloth that was tucked inside. I sure didn't want Mama to fade away again. Wasn't but one thing I could think of that made Mama smile no matter what bad things was happening. And that was stitching quilts.

LEAVING GEE'S BEND

Mama always said every quilt tells a story. Every piece of cloth, every stitch and every bit of cotton stuffed between the seams tells a secret about the one who made the quilt. And same as me, Mama sure does love a story.

Which is why I decided this next quilt—the one that so far was just pieces in my pocket—I was making that one for Mama. So no matter what happened with the baby, Mama would have my story to give her something to smile about. It'd be just big enough to wrap around Mama's shoulders when she sat in her rocking chair telling us stories before bed. And since I was making this quilt all about me, I was gonna make it *my* way.

I grinned. Wasn't a single thing Mama would be able to say about that.

Scraps

BY THE TIME I GOT MY EYE PATCH IN PLACE, MAMA was done collecting the eggs and had started to sweep the dirt yard with a broom she'd made out of sorghum stalks. Usually she would hum church hymns while she worked, but wasn't no humming today. Seemed like she was doing good just to get air flowing in and out.

I rubbed the goose bumps off my bare arms, then felt again in my pocket for my needle and cloth. Best I get started on that quilt right away. I crossed the yard on my tiptoes, careful not to make a mess of the clean lines Mama had just made in the dirt with the broom. Just as soon I got Delilah fed, I could pull out my needle and start stitching.

It was Mama that first taught me how to stitch. Just like her mama taught her. I still remember the first time she let me hold a needle with my own fingers. It was a few weeks after the accident that made my eye cloud over and stop seeing things. Wasn't nobody's fault about my eye. It was just a sliver of hickory that went flying from Daddy's ax, then had to go and land square in my eye.

I was a little bitty girl, not even in school yet. But I still remember the way my eye burned like it happened just this morning. And I remember how soon as I wasn't in pain no more Mama started teaching me all sorts of things. She'd rush through the washing, then sit down beside me.

"Them fields ain't the place for you, Ludelphia," Mama said. "Not with that eye." Mama pulled some scraps of cloth from her quilting basket. Most of 'em was ripped into squares. "You got to learn to do quiet things. Lady-like things."

Mama laid out a few pieces, then handed me the rest. "First thing you got to do is sort the colors. You puts the reds in one stack, the blues in another." She watched while I sorted. I didn't say nothing because it wouldn't have been ladylike, but I didn't see no point in sorting. Seemed to me some of the best things just happened with no order to 'em at all. But Mama, she believed in having a plan.

"That's good, Ludelphia. Real good. Now comes the hard part. You see this needle? It's real sharp, and I ain't got no thimble to fit your little finger. So you got to be careful." Mama held the needle between her finger and thumb as she licked the end of the thread. Then she handed 'em both to me. I'd watched her enough times to know the next thing I needed to do was push that thread right through the eye of the needle.

I may have only one eye that works, but I got to tell you, it works real good.

"It's like you was born to stitch," Mama said when she looked over my work. And I reckon I was. Ain't hardly a day passed since then that hasn't found me with a needle in my hand.

Trouble was, we didn't have no cloth except scraps. Wasn't no money for buying nothing new, so we made do with patched-up clothes until they was too small or too worn. It was like Christmas morning when Daddy's work britches finally gave out and Mama tore the faded denim into long strips.

But that was months ago. Which is why I wasn't in too big a hurry when I went out to feed Delilah. I searched the ground as I walked, hoping to find a stray piece of burlap or feed sack to put in my quilt.

Soon as she saw me pass the woodpile in the middle of our yard, Delilah started braying like there was no tomorrow.

"Hush up, Delilah! Don't want to make Mama mad.

Not today!" It didn't make no difference to Delilah that Mama was feeling bad. She kept up her racket until I got to the fence. Once I was there, she turned her ears forward and back, then stuck her nose through the fence for me to scratch. As I scooped grain from the feed sack, she nibbled my arms with her lips, her warm breath chasing away the cool autumn air. Soon as the feed was in her bucket, she buried her head and didn't pay me no more mind. I scratched her neck for a minute more as the sky began to lighten.

In the yard the hens squawked as Mama raised the broom and banged it against the side of the house to let all the dirt out of the sorghum stalks. Then she started beating it against the One Patch quilt she had strung up on the clothesline. Mama always said banging a quilt with the broom was just about the only way to keep the cloth clean in between washings. You knew you was done when those little clouds of dust stopped puffing up. But this time those little clouds sent Mama into another fit of coughing that forced her to stop and grab her knees again.

"You okay, Mama?" I hollered. She just nodded and waved me away. So I sank down to my spot on top of the feed sack and pulled out my needle. As Delilah crunched the grain between her teeth, I held my needle up in the air till it caught the light and started to shine. Not that I needed light to put in a good stitch. I could touch the knot with the tip of my tongue and know it was tight. I could trace them stitches with my fingers and know if they was straight or not. I didn't even have to think about what I was doing. When I was stitching, I could just let my mind go.

Once I got the needle started, I looked out at the little bit of the world you can see from my spot beside the barn. Wasn't much to it besides the half dozen cabins just like mine lined up side by side, so close to each other you could just about hear your neighbor's salt pork sizzling in the skillet.

In front of the cabins was a dirt footpath that led past Pleasant Grove Baptist Church and on to the cotton fields that took up most of Gee's Bend. Past the cotton fields was cornfields. And in the far-off distance was a row of pine trees that marked the edge of the swamp. Beyond the swamp, the dark waters of the Alabama River snaked through the trees, keeping me on one side and the rest of the world on the other.

What was it like across the river? Wasn't no way for me to know since I ain't never set foot outside of Gee's Bend. What I knew about was right here: this barn, this yard, this cabin. So when I heard banging sounds coming from inside, I knew my stitching time was just about up.

I tied a quick knot and had just got my needle put away when Daddy stomped down the wooden steps and into the yard. One look at the empty water bucket that was sitting on the ground next to the woodpile and I knew I had forgotten to draw the water. I real quick hopped off the feed sack and grabbed the handle. Daddy wouldn't like me stitching before I'd finished my chores.

"Reckon today we'll pull in what's left of the cotton. Then all we got left to do is haul it to the gin," Daddy said as he two-stepped across the yard. "Hallelujah!" Daddy's whole face sparkled. We was all looking forward to being done with the harvest. Then we could take it easy till planting time came around again.

Mama's lips curved into a half smile as she ran her hand across her big belly. "Make sure that boy does his share," she said as my brother, Ruben, eased out of the house. As if Ruben was still a little boy instead of an inch past Daddy. As if he'd ever been a lick of trouble in all his sixteen years.

"He knows I'll take the switch to him if I have to," Daddy said, giving Ruben a wink. Ruben grinned as he came down the steps without making a single one of them squeak. He was the only person I knew who could get into and out of our cabin without making a sound. Mama always said when Ruben wasn't being careful, he was being patient.

Mama never said those things about me. And it wasn't no secret that, unlike me, Ruben hadn't been switched in near about his whole life. He didn't say a whole lot, but you could count on him to do whatever you asked. He was born that way, I reckon. But there was things about Ruben Mama and Daddy didn't know. Things I found out by being neither patient nor careful.

Like how Ruben went fishing on Sunday afternoons, even when he knew as well as anybody Reverend Irvin said Sundays was for resting. The first time I followed Ruben out to the swamp, I gasped when I saw him pull a cane pole from behind a thick pine tree. Then, when he reached around another pine and pulled out a little tin bucket, I couldn't stop myself from talking.

"This is your big secret?" I said, coming out from my hiding spot behind a hydrangea bush. "Fishing?"

Ruben didn't jump or jerk, just turned to me like he knew I was there the whole time. "I reckon now it's *our* secret."

Wasn't but one other person that knew about me and

Ruben's secret, and that was Etta Mae Pettway from next door. She'd come out if it wasn't too hot. But that was before she went and moved off to Mobile. I reckon it'd been nearly a year since she fished with us.

Sometimes it seemed like them fish followed Etta Mae right out of Gee's Bend. I got tired of holding on to that pole when nothing was biting. So Ruben let me be in charge of digging worms out of the rich dirt under the pines. Then, when I was ready to try again, he'd bait my hook for me so I didn't have to be the one to kill those worms.

I swung the bucket by its handle as Ruben rocked back on his heels and Daddy gave Mama's shoulders a squeeze.

"You take it easy, you hear?" Daddy said as he rubbed Mama's arm. "Reverend Irvin said yesterday Mrs. Irvin will be by today with some onion broth. And won't be but a day or two till we finish up with the cotton. Then I'll be here to help, and the Pettways will too." Daddy glanced toward the Pettways' cabin next door. The Pettways was just like family, same as everybody else that lived in Gee's Bend. I reckon that's what happens when you work the same fields and go to the same church and live in cabins just about built on top of one another. "Looks like they beat us out this morning. Guess we better be getting on. Working in the far field today—good two-mile walk each way."

"I'm just so tired," Mama said, balling her hands into fists. "Cough won't let up and my back's been aching all morning."

"Don't you worry." Daddy kissed the top of Mama's head. "Everything's gonna be okay." Then he kissed the top of my head while Ruben kissed Mama's cheek. When he got to me, Ruben didn't kiss my cheek. He thumped my eye patch instead. Same as he always did. I don't reckon there was a better brother in the world than Ruben.

When they got to the chinaberry tree that marked the edge of the yard, Daddy turned back and hollered, "Lu, you mind your mama," Then he grinned that grin of his. Even when I didn't want to, I couldn't help but grin back.

Once they was gone, it got quiet in the yard again. I lifted the bucket onto my head and walked toward the spring that was tucked away in a little patch of poplar trees past the outhouse.

Just as I was turning the corner of the cabin, I heard a door slam shut and something yellow caught my eye. When you like to quilt, it's like your eyes is always on the lookout for color. Because it might be a scrap of cloth you can work into your quilt top. The yellow I saw that day was more than a scrap of cloth. It was a whole dress! And it was on a girl that was sitting on the porch steps of the Pettways' cabin next door.

Nobody had to tell me who it was. I knew right away.

Girl in the Yellow Dress

"ETTA MAE!" I SAID, DROPPING THE BUCKET IN THE dirt and running toward her. "I didn't know you was back!"

It was like the sky had opened up and poured sunshine out of a honey jar. Etta Mae Pettway was just about my favorite person in the whole wide world. At least she used to be, before she went to work a job in Mobile.

"Just now got here," Etta Mae said, her face hidden in the shadow of the front porch. "Missed the last ferry yesterday from Camden, so I had to wait for Willie Joe to cross over this morning."

The ferry was the quickest way in or out of Gee's Bend. Otherwise you had to walk up through Rehoboth and around about forty miles to get anyplace. And Willie Joe was the one that worked the ferry. Wasn't no getting across without Willie Joe's help.

"Where'd you sleep?" I said as I climbed the steps of the Pettways' cabin.

"On the riverbank in a pile of pinestraw. Same as you and me always did."

I grinned as my mind went back through all the sticky summer days me and Etta Mae waited on the riverbank while our mamas crossed the river to sell blackberries in Camden. Etta Mae was the one that watched after me and all the other children while our folks worked the fields.

Was I glad to see her! Ever since I was a little child, it was Etta Mae that helped me when I got myself into trouble. Like the time I stepped on a fire ant bed and got bites all over my legs. Anytime I got a fever or a rash of poison ivy, it was Etta Mae that stayed with me and rubbed mud on my itchy spots. She told me stories too. About things that happened in far-off places where there was deserts or snow or mountains so tall it took days to climb 'em.

Seemed like things hadn't been right ever since she'd been gone. Wasn't nobody else who'd take the time with things the way Etta Mae did. When she went off to Mobile to look after some white family's children, I wasn't sure she'd ever come back. And now here she was, standing right in front of me, like she ain't never left.

She looked just the same except for the dress. I ain't

never seen Etta Mae in anything other than a plain old sack dress just like mine. That yellow cloth sure wasn't made out of no fertilizer sack, that's for sure. I liked the way it set off her dark skin. I wanted to run and throw my arms around her same way as I always did, and tug at her hair that was caught up in them short braids she liked, the ones that always reminded me of blackberry brambles. But my legs just wouldn't move. Not when Etta Mae wasn't running toward me neither.

Hadn't been but a year since she left. What in the world could have happened to make her hang back in the shadows that way? Why wasn't she running out in the yard to be with me?

The air was suddenly cool again and nipped at my arms. I sank into my dress, wishing it had longer sleeves.

"Mercy, Ludelphia," Etta Mae said, finally coming out from under the eaves of the cabin. "You done shot up tall as a cattail since I've been gone." She wasn't telling me nothing I didn't already know. But I sure was glad she noticed! Maybe now she would throw her arms around me?

I leaned forward ever so slightly, but she still didn't reach her hands out. Set 'em right on her hips instead. Then she sat down on the top step and patted the seat next to her. "Might not have known you if not for that eye patch."

Real quick I scrambled up the steps. At least she was inviting me to sit with her. Our eyes met for just the briefest second before Etta Mae turned away. It was like she didn't know what to say to me. She seemed worried about something, nervous. And that made all them words I had stored up to say to her just disappear.

I smoothed my dress under my legs and sat down beside her. I couldn't count the times me and Etta Mae had sat beside each other on this very same step. I reckon I'd spent more time in my life with Etta Mae than with my very own brother, even though she and Ruben was the exact same age. Both of 'em, sixteen.

That's the way it was in Gee's Bend, the boys and men out working them fields, and most all of the women too. Ever since Etta Mae had been gone, I'd been the one to look after the little ones.

My mind was empty as a plate that had been licked clean. I couldn't think of anything to say, so I scratched under my eye patch, then reached up and felt my own hair. Mine was caught up in tight braids real close to my head.

My eye settled on Etta Mae's hands. How many times

had them thick knuckles braided my hair for me? Her hands was big, same as the rest of her. Not fat, but able to do anything. Seemed like wasn't nothing bad could happen when Etta Mae was around.

Underneath her hands the yellow cloth shined. Right away I started thinking about my quilt. What I would give for a piece of cloth like that! Etta Mae must have worked real hard to get such a fancy dress.

"You get that dress in Mobile?" I said, my hands folded together in my lap, when what I really wanted was to touch it and see if it was soft as it looked. But I didn't dare.

Etta Mae rested her hands on her knees. "You ain't heard what happened?" She looked me straight on for the first time, her forehead wrinkling from the top of her eyebrows all the way to where her hair started. "Aunt Doshie ain't been 'round talking about what Mrs. Cobb told Willie Joe?"

I shook my head. What could have happened in Mobile? "Aunt Doshie was here just yesterday, checking up on Mama. But I didn't hear her say nothing about you or Mrs. Cobb."

"You sure?" Etta Mae stood up and started walking across the yard toward my cabin. "Willie Joe said the only reason he was carrying me back over the river was because he'd told Aunt Doshie all about it, and he knew she'd warn folks about me."

Warn folks? About what? I didn't know what on earth Etta Mae was talking about. As I followed her the few dozen steps between her cabin and mine, my mind flipped but still turned up nothing.

When we got to the front porch stairs, Etta Mae squatted down and pointed underneath. "See that?" she said.

I tilted my head and strained my eye till I could see a dusting of white powder all over the ground. Wasn't no mystery to me what it was. It was devil's lye. For warding off evil spirits.

"You know how my mama is," I said. I made my voice light, like me and Etta Mae was just playing around same as we used to do. "She says it's best to be prepared. 'You just never know' is what she says. You remember, Etta Mae. Mama even keeps a flour sifter up under the mattress. Just in case some evil spirit gets in the house it'll be so busy counting them holes in the sifter that it'll plumb forget its business."

"I'm telling you, Lu. That devil's lye ain't there just for some old evil spirit."

What was Etta Mae getting at? "What do you mean?" I said. Wasn't nothing new about superstitions in Gee's

Bend. Most times we just laughed when Aunt Doshie would start up about "witch's corners" and how the dirt from the graveyard was bad luck. One time Etta Mae took all us children out to see the headstones and we loaded our pockets with that dirt. Ain't nothing bad ever happened.

When Etta Mae turned toward me, her dark eyes was bright and wet. Was that tears? There wasn't a time I could remember when I'd ever seen Etta Mae cry.

"Etta Mae?"

She sniffled and wiped her eyes with her fingers. "Ain't nothing," she said. "I'm just glad to be back in Gee's Bend where there ain't so much noise and confusion. Don't reckon I'll ever leave this place again."

"You trying to tell me you missed this place?" I fingered the ragged hem of my sack dress, then reached out and ran my finger along the smooth edge of Etta Mae's dress. "Where things is the same day after day, and there ain't no such thing as fancy clothes?"

Etta Mae's lips spread into a smile and a little laugh came out.

There was the Etta Mae I knew and loved. There was the face I remembered.

"Ain't but one thing I'm gonna miss about Mobile. And it's got nothing to do with dresses."

I leaned back on my elbows so I could watch her as she talked. "What then?"

"The missus, she had a piano. You should have seen it, Lu! The outside golden brown, like maple wood, only shiny? And them keys was so in tune it was like angels singing. Not like Reverend Irvin's broken-down church piano at all."

"Did you play it for the children? Same as you always done for me?"

"Sure did. It was just about the only way to get that baby to sleep. Me playing that piano."

The smile faded and Etta Mae took a step back. "Ludelphia, I got to tell you something." She shifted her weight from one foot to the other, then placed her hands on my shoulders like she wanted me to listen and she wanted me to listen good. "Bad things happened when I was in Mobile. Real bad things."

I held my breath. When my voice came, it was like a whisper. "What bad things?" It was like part of me wanted to hear what Etta Mae was about to say, but part of me didn't.

Just as she was opening her mouth to talk, Mama started up coughing from inside the cabin. One cough came right on top of the other, rough as Daddy's work britches against the washboard. Then there was a thump and the clatter of dishes hitting wood.

"Mama?" I said as I raced up the steps and into the cabin. I could hear Etta Mae following right behind me.

First thing I saw when I opened that door was Mama in a pile beside the kitchen table. She groaned, then let her head drop to the floor and didn't even try to get up.

Something Ain't Right

SOON AS I GOT TO MAMA, I CROUCHED DOWN BESIDE her. There was thick spit coming out the corner of Mama's mouth and a wet spot spreading along the floorboards next to her legs. Mama was leaking from both ends!

"Ludelphia," she said, her voice raw and broken, "I think it's the baby."

I touched Mama's forehead with the back of my hand as she closed her eyes and started to moan. The top of her nose was dotted with beads of sweat.

"It's too early," Mama said, squeezing her eyes shut. She didn't say it, but I knew she was thinking about them other babies.

"But your belly is a lot bigger this time, Mama."

Mama groaned. "Don't matter. It's still too soon."

It was like she had already given up. Like she expected the same thing to happen this time as before.

"But Mama. . . ." What she was forgetting was me. Me and Ruben. We'd come along just fine. Wasn't no reason this baby couldn't come along just fine too.

Etta Mae squatted beside me. "It's the baby coming, all right," she said, pointing to the wet floorboards. Now it was dripping through the slats onto the feathers and bits of cotton the chickens slept on at night. "Probably that mean cough is what brought it on. I seen this very thing happen when I was in Mobile."

Mama's eyes rolled under her lids the way they do sometimes when you're dreaming. Then all of a sudden they popped wide open. "Get on with you, Etta Mae!" Mama waved her arms in the air like Etta Mae was a fly that needed swatting. "Don't need your help. Just need Ludelphia."

I locked my eye on Etta Mae but didn't say a word.

So it was true. The devil's lye was set out for Etta Mae. Whatever those bad things were that happened in Mobile, Aunt Doshie had already spread the word. And now my mama was so scared she was sending away the very person who could help her.

Now what was I supposed to do?

As Etta Mae eased toward the door, Mama worked to get her feet up under her. But each time she got about halfway up, she'd sink back down again. Etta Mae and me looked at each other, our eyes wide. Why was Mama so weak?

"Don't go," I mouthed to Etta Mae, then watched as she slipped outside the screened door. Wasn't no sound of footsteps on the porch, so I knew she was staying close. I turned my attention back to Mama and tried to make my voice sound like Daddy's. "It's okay. Everything's gonna be okay."

One more time Mama tried to lift herself. When she fell back, she landed crooked. Her eyes popped open as she hit and there was a crunching sound.

"The eggs!" she said, her voice cracking. She dipped her hand into the pocket of her apron. When she pulled out her fingers, they was dripping with egg yolk. "Every one of 'em broken!"

Broken eggs meant no corn bread for supper. Broken eggs meant waking up in the middle of the night with a grumbly belly. I felt my shoulders slump. I should have collected them eggs myself. Instead of planning my quilt and worrying about my eye patch, I should have been helping my mama.

I blinked back tears. "It's okay, Mama." I reached around her back to untie the apron strings. "Don't you worry about them eggs." Because we got bigger things to worry about, is what I wanted to say. But wasn't no need to say such a thing. Mama was the one with weak legs and a cough and a baby ready to come out. Wasn't much of nothing I could tell Mama that she didn't already know.

Even though I knew Etta Mae was just out there on the porch, I ain't never felt so alone as I did right then. Didn't take but a few big steps to cross from one side of the cabin to the other, but did it ever feel empty with Mama stuck there on the floor.

I fingered the needle and scraps in my pocket. Mama always said wasn't but one way to do things, and that was one stitch at a time.

First I had to get them drippy eggs out of Mama's apron. As I scooped the yolks and whites into a wooden bowl, I imagined tearing Mama's calico apron into strips and laying 'em out to be the edges of the quilt I was making for Mama. All them reds and browns and greens would liven it right up.

When I was done with the eggs, I threw open the shutters to let some good light into the room. Then I hooked my arms under Mama's armpits. "Come on, Mama," I said as I pulled her toward the cornshuck pallet that was hers and Daddy's. Mama lifted her body some and groaned as she settled onto the bed. Then her breathing started coming fast and noisy and I knew from the times before that she was having birthing pains.

I grabbed her hands, even though mine was shaking. "I'm right here, Mama." But what good was that? I didn't have no idea what to do next.

As Mama's legs stiffened and she clenched her fists, I told myself that this is how it's supposed to happen. Ain't no way to get a baby out without pain. So I just kept talking to her, mumbling "it's okay, Mama, don't you worry" over and over again until the sounds joined together and it was like singing a song.

Only Mama wasn't singing. She didn't talk at all no more, and her breath only came in sharp bursts.

Then everything changed. Mama's legs got limp and her breathing slowed down. I knew from before it wouldn't be long before the pains came again. What I needed to do now was focus. Just fix my mind on something so I could start thinking straight. So I looked around the log walls of the cabin that was plastered with pieces of newspaper Daddy brought back with him from Camden. The *Wilcox Progressive Era*, it was called, on account we lived in Wilcox County, Alabama.

Wasn't enough paper to cover all the cracks in them walls, but I got to tell you, every little bit helped to cut down on the wind that liked to creep in when you was least expecting it. Daddy said soon as there was a little extra money, he'd bring us home some more newspaper so we'd have something new to look at.

My favorite picture was the one just behind Mama's head. It was an ad for "LADIES COATS As Low As $1.95" at W. E. Cook's Department Store in Camden. The lady in the picture was tall, and she was wearing high-heeled shoes. Wasn't hardly nobody in Gee's Bend that had shoes at all, much less ones fancy as that.

And that coat. I ain't never seen nothing like it, not in Gee's Bend. It was some sort of fur that went from the lady's neck all the way to her ankles. Could be rabbit or fox, Daddy said.

"Ludelphia!"

I jerked my eye away from the wall. Mama's face was scrunched up just like a rotten chestnut. She grabbed her belly and started to pant like a yard dog after it's been chasing a squirrel.

The pains was getting worse. I wrapped my arms around my middle and squeezed 'em tight against my dress. I ain't ready for this, is what I wanted to say. My throat tightened and my lips was trembling. Slowly I began to take tiny steps backward.

I had to get help from someplace. If only Mama

wanted Etta Mae! She was right there on our porch ready to help.

Wasn't no getting Daddy and Ruben or the Pettways, not with them cotton fields a good two miles away. Looked like the baby was coming too fast for that. The Reverend Irvin and Mrs. Irvin? They'd sure come if I asked 'em to, but wasn't no telling where they might be. If only I knew whether they was at the church or someplace else. Wasn't no telling how long it might take me to find 'em.

I scratched up under my eye patch. That left only one person. Not a real doctor, but the closest thing we had in Gee's Bend.

"Mama, I'll be right back. I'm just gonna run fetch Aunt Doshie." Even though I didn't really want to. Aunt Doshie was the one that came with her potions them other times when the babies died. Her potions that seemed about as worthless as the visions she was always going on about.

Mama grabbed my arm. "Ain't no time for that. Ain't got nothing to pay her with, nohow." I glanced over at Mama's apron. For a short second I was glad about the broken eggs. I was glad there wasn't no time and nothing to pay Aunt Doshie with.

"Then, Mama, we ain't got no choice. I'm bringing in Etta Mae."

"Ain't having no witch in my house, Ludelphia!"

Witch? I stomped my foot in frustration. "Mama! It's just Etta Mae!" Now was not the time to be taking Aunt Doshie's rumors for truth.

At the sound of her name Etta Mae poked her head inside the door.

"Mrs. Bennett," she said, "least let me bring up a pail of water. You gonna need it." Etta Mae didn't wait for an answer.

"Lord, Jesus!" Mama leaned her head back against the wall of the cabin as the pain eased up for a moment. She took two big breaths. "You trying to kill me, Lu?"

I gritted my teeth and pressed my lips together. "No, Mama." What I was trying to do was save her. And the baby.

Mama didn't say nothing more. Just lay there quiet for a minute with her eyes closed. I stroked the hair back from her damp forehead. She was burning up.

As Etta Mae came through the door, water sloshed out of the bucket onto the floor. She didn't pay it no mind, just set right to work dumping the water into the iron pot.

When she was finished, she wiped her hands across the front of her dress. "Lu, you stoke the fire while I check on your mama."

I jumped right up and started poking the fire. As the

embers caught new pieces of wood and the flame rose higher, my heart began to slow down a little. It felt good to finally be doing something useful.

Meanwhile Etta Mae took a closer look at Mama. If Mama noticed it wasn't me by her side, she didn't let on. She was too busy groaning as the pain took hold again. As Etta Mae tucked the quilt in around her shoulders, Mama wrinkled her nose and pushed her lips out like Delilah does when the hay has begun to mildew. Then she started taking short breaths like she'd just run clear across the cotton field.

"Something ain't right, Ludelphia," Mama said between breaths. "Something ain't right!" Mama's eyes darted around the room like she was searching for something but just couldn't find it noplace. Then she pulled her legs up toward her chest and started shaking so hard her teeth was rattling. I reckon on account of the fever.

"Need a good knife," Etta Mae said, turning away from Mama.

I took a deep breath and made my voice stay calm even though my insides was shaking just as fast as Mama's teeth. "What for?"

"To put under the bed. To cut the pain."

I ain't never heard of such a thing, but I nodded my head anyway and pointed toward the spot high in the wall where Mama kept the knife. The blade caught the sunlight and flashed like lightning when Etta Mae yanked it out of the wood. Next thing I knew, Etta Mae had pushed that knife deep into Mama's mattress where you couldn't see it no more.

"Everything's okay, Mama," I said, even though at that moment I wasn't sure it was true.

I studied the pot of water. Steam was just starting to rise. "Water will soon be ready, Mama." The one thing I did know about was what to do with the water. "Then we'll wipe you down so everything's good and clean for the baby." I swallowed. "And when the baby comes, we'll wipe it down too."

Mama didn't make no reply except to start up with a new round of coughing that jolted her body in an unnatural way. I couldn't watch no more, so I let my head hang down until I was looking through the floorboards at the chickens.

I wanted to cry. I want to blink and have it all be over.

"Ludelphia," Etta Mae said, "now, you know there's gonna be some blood, right?" She waited for me to nod. "Just the way it is when babies come. Don't you worry about it none. You just do what I say and everything's gonna be just fine."

I nodded again and felt my shoulders relax. After all these years, I was used to Etta Mae telling me what to do.

"Get two good quilts," she said. "Put one up under her legs, keep the other one down near her feet. That one will be for the baby."

From the stack next to the door I pulled Mama's favorite Housetop quilt and an old Nine Patch pattern that was ripped in places. Just as I was getting Mama's legs settled on top of the old Nine Patch, Mama got quiet and sat straight up in bed. Her eyes was open, but they was blank as the chalkboard on the first day of school.

"Lord, Jesus," Mama said in a loud, clear voice, "I'm coming home!" Wasn't no mistaking them words. Mama reached out her arms like she was gonna hug somebody. But there wasn't nobody there. Just me waiting at the foot of the bed and in between us nothing but air.

"Big Mama? That you?" Mama said, her eyebrows raised and the whites of her eyes shot with little red lines. Then she grabbed hold of my wrist. Her fingers clamped down so tight wasn't no way for blood to get to my fingers. Just as they was starting to tingle, Mama all of a sudden turned me loose.

"No, Mama." I rubbed my wrist with the fingers on my other hand. "It's just me, Ludelphia. Ain't nobody else here."

I looked at the door where I knew Etta Mae was waiting and thought, What if it was true? I thought about how she yanked that knife out of the wall, then shoved it up under Mama's mattress. What if she really was a witch and her being here was making things worse, not better?

"Big Mama?" Mama said again, her eyes wide open but not seeing nothing. Big Mama? The only Big Mama I knew of was the one from Mama's stories. But she'd been dead for at least a hundred years. It was like my mama had gone and lost her mind. Then she started moaning so loud I knew I didn't have no choice. Witch or not, I needed Etta Mae.

"Etta Mae!" My voice came out high like a pig squeal. "She don't even know who I am!"

I couldn't hardly breathe as Etta Mae pushed in front of me and went right to Mama's head. It was like all the air had disappeared and the cabin wasn't no bigger than the outhouse with the door closed.

Etta Mae leaned over Mama and talked in her ear. "This here is Big Mama. You hear? Big Mama wants you to push now. Bear down just as hard as you can."

Right away, Mama grabbed the quilt in her fingers and squeezed so hard I could see all the bones in her hands, like they was gonna pop right out of her skin. She ground her teeth together and squeezed her eyes so tight they seemed to disappear.

"Ludelphia!" Etta Mae hollered. "It's time to catch the baby! It's gonna be all slippery, so you got to hold tight."

Mama's face was shiny now, and the sweat was dripping down her neck. Her hair was plastered against her head, and she was still shaking. Etta Mae kept talking in a low voice that sounded almost like a cat's purr. I couldn't hear a word she was saying, but it didn't matter. Not when whatever she was saying made all the lines in Mama's face ease up.

"Now, Ludelphia!" Etta Mae cried. "Baby's coming now!"

Mama screamed. She screamed so loud I thought Daddy and Ruben might come running in from the fields to see what the matter was. But even if they had been right outside the door instead of two miles away, they wouldn't have been quick enough. I held out my hands just in time for a small, waxy brown body to slide between Mama's bony legs right into my arms.

Baby Rose

FOR THE FIRST FEW SECONDS THERE WASN'T NO noise except the popping of the fire. Even Mama was quiet. The baby didn't flip or flop the way fish do when you pull 'em out of the water. It was completely still.

"Rub the chest!" Etta Mae said as she turned the baby's head and used a finger to clear the gunk out of its mouth.

"You got to breathe, baby!" I said as I used the bright orange corner of the Housetop quilt to rub firm circles against the small chest till finally the baby sputtered and coughed. Etta Mae real quick pulled the baby up to her shoulder and banged her hand against the baby's back. Then the baby began to squall.

I ain't never heard a sound as good as that one. This baby wasn't like all them other ones. This baby was alive.

"She's gonna be just fine," Etta Mae said as she laid the baby on its back beside Mama.

She? I grinned. I ain't told nobody, but I had really been hoping for a girl. And Mama ain't never said so, but I knew it was what Mama wanted too. Because when she pulled out the small wooden box of baby things from behind the bed, it was the pink gown she held up in the air then pressed close to her heart.

"Look, Mama!" I said, shaking her shoulder with my free hand. She lay there limp as a sack of sugar, so I shook her again. "Mama, wake up and meet your new baby girl!"

Mama rolled her head from one side to the other. "A girl?"

"That's right, Mama. Just what you wanted." Mama dipped her chin into her shoulder and smiled a small smile, but she didn't open her eyes. I reckon after all that I'd be tired too.

Etta Mae reached under the mattress and fumbled around for the knife. "Next we got to cut the cord."

I knew about that part too. So I held the baby with one arm and stretched out the cord with the other. Etta Mae made one quick cut, and Mama and baby was split apart for good.

As Etta Mae bundled up the baby, I wiped the sweat

from Mama's face. That's when I saw a little bit of blood coming out of the corner of Mama's mouth. And specks of it along her left cheek.

I didn't have no idea why blood was coming out of Mama's mouth. But I knew it needed to be cleaned, so I used the quilt to wipe the dark red spots away.

Mama's eyes moved under her eyelids. "I can't," she began in a voice that was barely a whisper.

I moved my ear close to her mouth so I'd be sure to hear. "Mama. You got to talk louder." But Mama didn't answer. She just lay there shivering, with her breath making that rattling sound again.

Etta Mae stood next to the fire where she'd been dipping old quilt strips into the steaming water to help clean the baby. "She still out of her head?"

I placed my hand on Mama's chest and watched it move up and down. "Just tuckered out, I reckon." It bothered me that she didn't want to hold the baby right away. But I knew what Mama had just done was at least as hard as a sun-baked July day in the fields. Anybody would be tired after all that.

"Come on, then, and see your baby sister."

I found Mama's hand and gave her fingers a squeeze. Then I took the baby from Etta Mae.

It was like the best Christmas ever, holding that brand-new baby. Her nose and eyes and each little dimpled finger was so small and perfect. Just a few minutes before, she'd been hidden away inside Mama, and now here she was, a real live person.

I stroked the baby's smooth cheek. "Can you believe it, Etta Mae?" Her body sure was long compared to the fatness of her face.

Etta Mae didn't say nothing, just gave a crooked smile and reached out a finger to touch the baby's fuzzy black hair.

I didn't have no idea what Mama was planning to name the baby, but looking at her, I knew just what I'd call her. "Rose," I said as the baby moved its mouth toward my finger. "She looks just like one of them climbing roses by the spring."

"Need to bury the afterbirth next," Etta Mae said as she put the dirty quilts in a pile next to the door. Her movements was quick and sure, like she did this sort of thing every day. "I'll set it out there behind the barn on my way out. And you'll have to wash them quilts. But first put on a pot of peas! Your daddy and Ruben is gonna be hungry when they get home. And soon as I'm gone, see if you can get her to wake up a little. Baby needs to meet her mama."

And then like a ghost Etta Mae was gone.

All My Fault

SEEMED LIKE IT WASN'T NO TIME BEFORE THE chickens started squawking as Daddy and Ruben came across the yard. I rushed out onto the porch soon as I heard them.

"Daddy! Ruben! Wait till you see!"

As Daddy's face crinkled in confusion, I rushed back into the cabin where the smell of peas and fried salt pork made the room warm and inviting. The cabin seemed smaller, too, what with Reverend and Mrs. Irvin standing next to Mama's bed. But I sure was glad they was there.

Reverend Irvin was so tall it was like watching a pine sapling bend in the wind as he prayed over Mama. And there was a softness to his face that made you feel like wasn't no way he could hurt nobody. I reckon it was good that he was married to Mrs. Irvin because she was 'bout as wide as he was tall. They didn't have no children of their own, but it was like Mrs. Irvin's hips was made for holding babies. I ain't never seen her eyes so bright as when she had a little one in her lap.

I held my breath as Daddy pushed open the door. I didn't have no idea what he would say, but I sure wanted to be there to hear it.

"Well, I'll be," Daddy said as he walked inside to see Mrs. Irvin standing by the fire with a bundle in her arms. From his place next to Mama's bed, Reverend Irvin stopped his praying and gave Daddy a nod.

I couldn't hold back no longer. "The baby came early, Daddy!" I said, still holding the wooden spoon I'd been using to stir the peas. Wasn't right for anybody to tell him but me. "And it's a girl, Daddy. A healthy baby girl!" I wrapped my arms around Daddy's waist and squeezed hard as I could. He felt so good and solid, like a water oak rooted in the clay dirt next to the river. "First Mama was coughing so bad she just about couldn't stand up, then the birthing pains started, and Daddy, the baby is fine, just fine!" I looked up at him. "Not like them other times at all."

"Well, I'll be," he said again, his voice turned tender. I let my hands drop from his waist so he could move closer to the baby. Daddy patted my head, then wiped his hands across his britches before reaching out a finger to touch the baby's cheek.

After he looked at her for a while, he turned to me and grinned. Then he looked past me where Ruben was still standing next to the door, quiet as could be.

"Come on now, Ruben," Daddy said, motioning with his hand for Ruben to come forward. "Meet your baby sister."

Ruben's face just about glowed as he took one slow step after another toward the baby.

"How do you like that, son?" Daddy chuckled as Ruben finally got to where Mrs. Irvin stood holding the baby. "Finish pulling in the cotton and get a new baby on the very same day!"

"She sure is little," Ruben said, shoving his hands in his pockets. He stood like that for a minute, just looking. Then he reached over and thumped me on the eye patch. "Just what we needed, another little girl."

We all laughed then, and Daddy rubbed the top of my head. "Some kind of day you had, Lu." I could feel my insides getting all warm. Wasn't all the time Daddy gave me praise in front of other folks.

"And how's the new mother?" Daddy motioned toward Mama, and Reverend Irvin shifted out of the way so Daddy could get a good look.

Reverend Irvin cleared his throat. "Not doing so good, I'm afraid." He stood back as Daddy ran his finger along Mama's ear and jaw. "She's either coughing like it's gonna break her in half or sleeping so hard nothing will wake her."

Daddy bit his lip, then cocked his head. "Reckon the baby coming made the coughing worse?"

"Not rightly sure," Reverend Irvin said.

"Mrs. Irvin?" Daddy said, turning his head toward her.

Mrs. Irvin tucked the quilt under the baby's chin but didn't stop her swaying. Then she looked up at Daddy. "You know how it is when babies come," she said. "She's probably just wore out. That coughing sure don't help, but give her a day or two and I reckon she'll be back to her old self."

Daddy sat on the corner of the pallet, his big thumbs stroking the top of Mama's hand. Her hands was so thin and fragile-looking next to Daddy's wide ones that had scars zigzagging across the knuckles. "Thank you, Reverend Irvin. Mrs. Irvin," he said, looking from one to the other. "Go on home now. Ain't no sense you being here when you got families waiting for you to visit." Daddy looked from me to Ruben. "We can handle it from here."

Soon as they was gone, Daddy went into the kitchen

and started serving up the peas and corn bread. I ain't never seen him do that. Wasn't a time I could remember when Mama wasn't well enough to do it herself. Even when she lost them other babies, she still got on up and fed us supper.

While I got the baby settled in the little pallet Mrs. Irvin had made for her at the foot of Mama's bed, Ruben got busy hauling in enough split logs to keep the cabin warm all night. Mama just lay there curled in a ball, her breath coming in and out like a March wind.

Once we was all gathered around the table and the blessing had been said, Daddy took a few bites, then blotted his mouth with a napkin. "Lu?" he said. "Tell us how it all happened."

So I told him how Mama fell to the ground when I was over talking to Etta Mae. I told him about the puddle of water and how Mama coughed and shook and just about lost her mind. "If it wasn't for Etta Mae, I don't know what I'd have done," I said.

Daddy's eyes was like knives. "Lu, did you let Etta Mae into this house?"

"Yessir." I held my breath, remembering what Mama said before about Etta Mae being a witch. "I didn't know what else to do."

Daddy sighed then. The kind of sigh grown folks

make when they hear something they don't want to hear, but there's not a thing they can do about it. Like when Daddy heard the news from Reverend Irvin that cotton prices was down to a nickel a pound after being high as forty cents in years past. Price just kept on dropping farther down. Wasn't nothing to be done about it, but it was still right disappointing.

"I wish you hadn't done that, Lu." Daddy hung his head and shook it from side to side. "Your mama . . . your mama's gonna have a fit when she hears. Anything that goes wrong now, she'll blame Etta Mae." Daddy looked up at me, then pushed hard against the table. His chair scraped the floorboards till it got lodged in one of the cracks. Supper was over, and Daddy hadn't even eaten all his peas.

It was all my fault. I was the one that let Etta Mae in, even when Mama said not to. "I'm sorry, Daddy." I swallowed hard to hold the tears back. "You and the Pettways was way off in the fields, and there wasn't time to get Aunt Doshie." I picked at a stray thread in the hem of my dress and pulled it till it popped. "Etta Mae was the only one I could call. And you know she's helped with babies being born before. When she was in Mobile. Daddy, she knew just what to do."

"Don't matter, Lu. Don't know if she's a witch or

cursed or what have you, but one sure thing, that girl's got some awful bad luck. Death follows her around like a half-starved dog." Daddy stood up and put his hands on his hips. "Look at your mama, Lu."

I cut my eye in Mama's direction, but I couldn't look. It was enough just to hear her struggling to breathe.

Daddy shook his head. "Don't need none of that up in here. Just don't need it."

I wanted to slink through the floorboards like an old rat snake. Just slither out and never come back. Part of me wanted to say I'm sorry over and over, to beg him to forgive me, but the other part of me wanted to scream, Daddy, you wasn't here! I'm only ten years old—how on earth was I supposed to know what to do?

But then the weight of Daddy's words settled in.

Death. Daddy was worried about death.

I looked over at Mama and saw her this time, really saw her. How small she looked. How her chest heaved.

What if I was wrong about everything? What if by letting Etta Mae into the cabin, I had let in death?

The baby whimpered and squirmed till one of her arms got free of the quilt Mrs. Irvin had swaddled her in.

Before Daddy or Ruben had a chance to even move, I jumped up and pulled her into my arms. She was as warm and alive as any creature could be. "Shhh, Rose," I said, pulling her to my chest. I swayed her in my arms just the way I'd seen Mrs. Irvin do. "Hush now, Rose."

"Rose, huh?" Daddy said, his face softening. He got up from the table and with his big fingers pulled the blanket away from the baby's face. "Ain't she something?" He stared at her so long my arms was starting to ache. "Rose," he said. "Sweet little Rose. Wait till your mama gets a good look at you! She'll be so busy just looking at you, the rest of us will have to pick up the slack."

He ran his finger over Rose's tiny lips, then looked over at me and Ruben when Rose began to pucker up. His eyes was wet and shiny. "Best thing we can do is get this baby fed, then try to get some sleep. Your mama's gonna need us to be extra strong for her and little Rose."

"Yessir," Ruben and me said at the very same time. We laughed together, and I imagined someday Rose would laugh with us too. In just one day, our family had grown from two children to three. It was sure gonna take some getting used to.

Soon as it was dark, Daddy lit the lamp and set it beside Mama's bed. "Best get some rest." Daddy looked from Mama to Rose, then back at me. "Lu, you keep the baby with you, and me and Ruben will take turns watching over Mama."

I got to look after the baby? This day sure was full

of surprises, because I ain't never done nothing like that before. Not even when there was a new calf. Mama always said things like that was Ruben's job. So I real quick snuggled Rose close to me and sat with her on the little pallet at the foot of Mama's bed. Rose just lay there sleeping, quiet and peaceful.

In the lamplight I could see the lump of mama's apron still in a pile on the floor. First thing tomorrow morning I'd get it washed and hung on the line so it would be ready for Mama when she got all better.

I thought about the quilt I was making for Mama. I pictured my needle going in and out of a piece of that calico, with its reds and browns and greens. All I needed was just a small piece to tell this part of my story. Wouldn't take nothing more than the tail of the sash to get four good strips of cloth. I could stitch 'em in right along the edge of the quilt—one for me, one for Etta Mae, one for Mama and one for Rose. Wouldn't be no trouble at all and Mama wouldn't mind none soon as I showed her the quilt.

My eyelids began to get heavy, so I let them close. My breathing got slow and regular, and I could tell I was almost asleep.

I jerked when Mama started up coughing again. The sound was hard and hollow. The cough came on strong and steady for a while, then it stopped. But it always came back, jolting me from sleep. Between that awful cough and Rose's sudden cries, not a one of us slept good that night. We was too busy worrying.

As dawn peeked through the cracks in the cabin walls, Daddy and me and Ruben gathered around Mama. Her eyes was glued shut with some sticky mess and her skin was burning with fever. The quilt was soaked from Mama's sweat, and the cough had turned weak and dry. She looked so old and worn lying there, not like my mama at all.

"Lu," Daddy said finally, his voice thick, "go check to see if Mama's got some corn or something stored up in the barn. And, Ruben, run on over and fetch Aunt Doshie." He didn't even look up when he said it, just kept looking at Mama and stroking her hand.

As we stepped away from the bed, Daddy leaned in even closer to Mama. "You got to get better, you hear?" Daddy's voice cracked at the end, so I knew he was hiding tears. He let go of Mama's hands and ran his fingers over his stubbly chin. Then he sighed another one of them sighs that seemed to go on forever.

Wait and See

WHEN I GOT TO THE WOODPILE, I COULD SEE Delilah was waiting for me, same as always. She brayed soon as she saw me.

"Morning, Delilah," I said when I got to her. I scratched around her ears and she nuzzled my chest. Must be nice to be a mule, with no more to worry about than when the food was coming. I dumped grain into her bucket, then swung open the heavy barn door and breathed in real deep. I could feel my shoulders let loose and my chest open up. I'd always liked the smell of old hay and fresh manure.

I walked over to the far corner of the barn where Mama stored the vegetables. Wasn't nothing in the corn bin, so I pulled open the potato bin. Way in the back was two puny sweet potatoes. They wasn't much bigger than my hands, but they was still firm. Just right for boiling and mashing.

I reckon Mama had been saving them potatoes to pay Teacher on the first day of school. With the cotton harvest almost all done, school would be starting early as next week.

I sighed as I put 'em in my pocket. Now there wouldn't be nothing to give Teacher for coming all the way from Camden.

Then again, could be Mama had something else stored up that nobody knew about. Something else that would be just right for Teacher. Like last Thanksgiving when the food was all set out and we was just about to say the blessing and Mama said, "Wait. Everybody close your eyes." When we opened 'em, there was a fat, ripe tomato sitting in Mama's hand! Like it was August instead of November.

She'd wrapped that tomato in newspaper and buried it in the dirt behind the barn. Not a one of us knew about it till she held it out, then sliced it up and put it on the table. Didn't matter that it was soft and a little mealy. It was a fresh tomato when everything else had long since been blanched and preserved, then stored in jars on a shelf in the barn.

Soon as I got the barn door closed up and the latch in place, I settled onto the ground and pulled out my needle and thread. The sooner I got my quilt top stitched, the sooner I could set it in a frame and finish it for Mama.

I put in three rows of stitches before I saw Aunt Doshie walking down the footpath from her cabin to ours, her small body tucked up against Ruben's side. Don't know why everybody called her "aunt." She wasn't no taller than me, and far as I knew, she didn't belong to nobody. She took short steps and leaned on the cane as she walked, her long gray hair swinging in a braid behind her.

Ruben nodded his head when he saw me looking. I nodded real quick, then held my stitching up close to my face so Aunt Doshie wouldn't see me looking.

Wasn't no telling the things Aunt Doshie had been saying to him during the mile walk over. Seemed like she had something to say about everybody that lived in Gee's Bend. Which is why it didn't matter much that we didn't get no newspaper in Gee's Bend. Not with Aunt Doshie around to spread the word.

Soon as they passed me, I tucked away my needle and followed behind. I wanted to be there to hear what Aunt Doshie had to say about Mama.

Please, Aunt Doshie, I silently begged. Do something to make Mama's coughing and shaking go away. Whatever it takes. Make Mama well and I promise I'll wear my eye patch every day, just the way Mama wants me to.

Next thing I knew, Ruben was stumbling and Aunt Doshie was standing stock-still. Then she turned herself around and stared at me hard.

Had she heard my mind talking?

The eyelid under my eye patch started to twitch. Wasn't natural, her looking at me like that. It made me want to run into the woods and hide out by the swamp.

She knew. Aunt Doshie took one look at me and she knew without anybody even saying it that it was all because of me. I was the one responsible for Mama being sick. Because I was the one that let Etta Mae in.

Dear Lord, what was she gonna say about Mama?

As Daddy introduced Aunt Doshie to baby Rose, I took the potatoes from my dress pocket and placed 'em on the table. Then I picked Mama's apron from off the floor so I could get it washed up.

"Baby looks good and healthy," Aunt Doshie said as Daddy squeezed milk from a washcloth into Rose's mouth. "Now let's take a look at her mama."

As Aunt Doshie pulled back the quilt, Mama groaned and shifted in the bed. "Easy now, easy now," Aunt Doshie said, like she was talking to a fidgety milk cow.

Mama had sweat so much you could see right through her clothes. I wanted to cover her right back up again because I knew Mama wouldn't like folks seeing her like that. But Aunt Doshie was in charge now.

Aunt Doshie felt Mama's head and ran her fingers along her neck and behind her ears. She bent close to look in Mama's eyes, but some of the lashes was stuck together with yellow crust. When she got to Mama's mouth, she ran her finger across the dry cracked lips. Then she turned to Daddy. "Has she been coughing blood?"

Blood? I could feel my face get warm as Daddy answered.

"I seen some this morning," Daddy said, swallowing hard. "But none before that. It's just been yellow spit till now."

It wasn't true. I'd wiped blood from Mama's mouth yesterday, way back when Rose was first born. But I couldn't say it.

"Hmmm." Aunt Doshie creased her brow, then leaned over and put her ear on Mama's chest. "Looks to be the same as what Allie Bendolph was suffering with before she passed." The room fell silent as Daddy and Aunt Doshie looked hard at one another.

Was Aunt Doshie saying that Mama was gonna die? Just like old Mrs. Bendolph did? It felt like my throat was closing up. Like any second I wasn't gonna be able to breathe.

Aunt Doshie shook her head and drew her mouth into a thin line. "I'm sorry, Mr. Bennett." She folded her arms across her chest and stepped away from Mama. "But it don't look good."

"It's influenza, then?" Ruben said, his voice small and quiet.

Aunt Doshie leaned against her cane. "Looks like it. And with her chest rattling the way it is, and the fever hanging on so long . . . reckon she's got herself a touch of pneumonia too."

Daddy covered his ear and fixed his eyes on Rose. He didn't say a word, not one. So the rest of us didn't neither. It was like the news was so awful he had to block it out of his mind. Like if he didn't hear Aunt Doshie say it, then it couldn't be true.

But I had heard Aunt Doshie loud and clear. Influenza. Pneumonia. Them words was bigger than I was. And folks right here in Gee's Bend had died because of them words. Wasn't no more than two weeks ago that we'd sat through Mrs. Bendolph's funeral. One Sunday she was in church, the next she was dead.

It couldn't be right what Aunt Doshie was saying. Wasn't nothing new, folks dying. But not my mama.

"Aren't you gonna help her, Aunt Doshie?" I said. "Aren't you gonna do something?"

"Ain't nothing to be done here. Except wait and see."

"What do you mean?" I said. There had to be something Aunt Doshie could do. "Don't you have some potions or something?" I looked from her to Daddy. "You have to do something. Aunt Doshie, Mama would want you to at least try!"

Aunt Doshie narrowed her eyes and pointed her finger at me. "Now don't you sass me. Not after what you done."

It was like she had taken a switch to me. What if it really was my fault?

From the pallet, Mama started coughing. Small coughs at first, but they grew into coughs so big they pulled her head right off the pillow.

Aunt Doshie put her hand on Daddy's shoulder. "You got to keep everything clean. Don't want to be passing this to nobody else." She smoothed Rose's hair with her fingers. "And give her as much water as she'll take. Dribble it in her mouth same way you done with the baby."

She looked over at Ruben, who was staring into the fire. "Ruben, you boil up some water and pour it in a bowl. Then set that bowl on your mama's chest." Aunt Doshie pointed to the spot right below Mama's chin. "Right here.

But be careful so you don't burn her, you hear? Then cover her head and the bowl with a quilt. Like a little tent. The steam will loosen up her chest so her breath can come easier."

Aunt Doshie turned back to Mama and used the corner of the quilt to wipe her mouth. "And watch for more blood. If she starts coughing a stream of blood, you'll know it's in the Lord's hands. Ain't nothing left to do then but pray."

It felt like there was a bag of fertilizer on my chest. I was the only one that knew just how long Mama had been coughing blood. Even though it wasn't no stream of blood the way Aunt Doshie was saying.

"Daddy?" I said, my voice quivering as tears slid down my throat. I wanted him to wrap his big arms around me. I wanted him to tell me everything was gonna be okay. That it wasn't as serious as Aunt Doshie was making it out to be.

But Daddy wouldn't look at me. He just shook his head and stared at the floor.

The cabin began to spin around me till nobody was left but me. The room was silent and spinning, and I was alone in a place I ain't never been before. If I didn't get out of that room I was gonna bust right open like a watermelon that's gone too ripe.

"Got to go do the washing," I said. Never mind that Mama had done all the washing the day before. There was still the apron and quilts to tend to.

Was it only yesterday that Rose was born? Seemed like weeks had passed.

I made my way toward the barn where Delilah stood in her spot next to the feed bucket, her eyes half closed. Dust mingled with the flies that was swarming around her hooves. Even in the cooler weather, them flies wouldn't let her be.

While Delilah stomped and swished her tail, I leaned my head against the place on her shoulders where the hair was thin from being hooked to the plow. "What are we gonna do, Delilah?" I pressed my nose into her hair. She smelled just the way fishing worms do when you first pull 'em out of the ground. I breathed in deep and felt in my pocket for my needle and scrap of cloth.

"I tell you what you gonna do." I lifted my head and peeked over Delilah's back.

Etta Mae!

I let my breath out real slow. Etta Mae didn't know how bad things had gotten. "Aunt Doshie says ain't nothing we can do now except wait."

"That's what you think you should do, Ludelphia? Wait?" Etta Mae gave a little snort.

"You got any better ideas? Something like taking a knife out of the wall and shoving up under somebody 'to cut the pain'?" I threw my shoulders back. "If you hadn't come back, I wouldn't have had to go against my mama and let a witch into my house."

I took a step forward. Then another. What if that knife was some kind of curse? Who ever heard of such a thing, anyhow? If not for Etta Mae, Mama might not even be sick. "And now you gonna tell me what I need to do?"

She flinched. "That's right, Ludelphia. You got to go get your mama a real doctor. Like they should have done when that piece of hickory landed in your eye."

I rocked back on my heels. What was Etta Mae talking about? I gave my head a little shake, trying to clear it. "This ain't about my eye, Etta Mae. It's about you. And it's about Mama." I put my hands on my hips, and we was both quiet for a second as my mind tried to catch up.

"Besides," I said, "ain't no real doctors in Gee's Bend. You know that."

Delilah nudged my elbow with her nose. She could always tell when I was upset.

"But they got one in Camden. Name's Doc Nelson. Got himself an office right on Broad Street."

"Camden?" I gave Delilah another pat, then felt for my eye patch. It was right where it was supposed to be.

"Etta Mae, ain't no way Mama's gonna let me go to Camden." Beneath my fingers, Delilah's skin twitched.

"I don't reckon she can stop you."

The blood rushed to my head all at once, and things got real clear. Etta Mae didn't have a thing in the world to worry about. She was nearly grown, and she'd been to Mobile and back. She had a yellow dress, and her mama was good and healthy. And she was telling me I should go to Camden?

Tears sprung up in my good eye, so I swiped 'em away. I almost reached for Etta Mae's neck. I wanted to choke her! That way she couldn't say one more word about my mama.

But no matter how much I'd grown, my hands was too small for her neck. So I did the next best thing. I made fists and I beat against that yellow dress till my arms got tired. Etta Mae stood there solid as a stump against my blows.

Tears streamed down my face, and I started to hiccup. I let my arms hang down. Just rested my head on Etta Mae's chest and sobbed. After a minute she put her hand on my head and stroked my braids. Same way Mama always did.

"You done now?" she said.

Nodding, I took a step back and wiped my nose on my

sleeve. "Why don't you just tell me the truth, Etta Mae. Is you a witch or ain't you?"

The glow faded, and Etta Mae's eyes got even darker than they usually was. "I wish I knew, Ludelphia. I wish I knew."

The Storm

IT RAINED HARD THAT NIGHT, FOR THE FIRST TIME IN weeks. Rain dripped through the cracks in the roof, then dripped onto the chickens that was roosting under the floorboards. For a while it rained so hard there wasn't no point even trying to talk over the racket it made. Wasn't no way to keep dry neither.

The wetness wasn't as bad as the smell. I draped a Hog Pen quilt over my head to keep out the stench of wet feathers and quilts ripe with Mama's sickness. To keep my mind off it, I breathed through my mouth and tried my best to keep my needle moving. Put in one row of stitches, then another.

All the while I was turning over and over the things Etta Mae said about going to Camden and getting a real doctor for Mama.

Was it possible? I mean, for *me*?

If only Mama'd let me go with her one of them times she'd gone across the river to sell blackberries. Then I'd know better what to do. I'd know what to expect.

I reckon I was waiting for a sign. For something to happen that would tell me to go or not go.

"How is she?" I said, holding my needle still for a moment.

"'Bout the same," Daddy said. He was holding the steam tent over Mama's face, just like Aunt Doshie said. It seemed to make her breath come easier for a little while, but soon as the bowl and quilt was gone she'd get to rattling again. Hadn't stopped her eyes from crusting over neither. And she hadn't eaten a bite all day, not even the broth Daddy tried to dribble between her dry, cracked lips. It just dripped down the side of her neck. But Daddy kept on trying, even in the rain. He wasn't one to give up.

"Need the umbrella," Ruben said when he pulled the quilt away and a raindrop found Mama's face. As Ruben moved the steam bowl from Mama's chest, Daddy pulled Mama's umbrella from behind the bed. Mama kept that umbrella for nights just like this one. I reckon there wouldn't be no need for an umbrella if we wasn't so behind paying back what Mr. Cobb done loaned us. Then Daddy could have fixed that roof.

I sighed. Could things get any worse? I wanted to go back to them times like the one when Daddy brought that umbrella home from Camden Mercantile. I reckon I must have been about six years old because it was about the time I first started to school.

"Got something for you," Daddy said, holding the umbrella behind his back.

"Hush, now," Mama said, like she thought he was just teasing her. Then Daddy twirled the umbrella around and held it out for her.

Mama gasped and her eyes got real big. "I won't have to wear my rain hat no more!" She pushed the umbrella high as it would go in the cabin, like she was testing it out in a real rain. Then she set it on her shoulder and spun around.

Mama loved that umbrella, all right. Didn't bother her a bit when I told her what Teacher said about it being bad luck to open an umbrella in the house. She said it was worse luck to get soaked when you was sitting in your very own home.

I reached for Rose, even though it wasn't feeding time and she wasn't making a peep. I wanted to feel like I was helping. Only I was tired of doing the same old chores in the same little yard and the same four walls.

I thought about Etta Mae telling me I should go to Camden to get Doc Nelson. That would sure be different.

I pulled the quilt tighter around my shoulders. "What's it like in Camden?"

"Not as good as Gee's Bend," Ruben said, still holding the umbrella over Mama.

"It's just different, that's all," Daddy said. "Got things there we ain't got here. Like the Wilcox Hotel. And now on the corner right next to it, Mr. Dunn just opened up a Gulf Service Station. For folks to stop and put gasoline in them fancy motorcars."

"Don't need no service station here," Ruben said. "Don't need no hotel neither."

"Etta Mae said they got a doctor. That maybe he could help Mama."

"Well, sure they got a doctor. Just like we got Aunt Doshie," Daddy said. "Lu, didn't you hear what Aunt Doshie said? Ain't nothing we can do that we ain't already doing." Daddy dropped his head. "Besides, can't pay no doctor with sweet potatoes."

"Reckon Mr. Cobb would help us?" I said. "Reckon he'd loan us the money to pay the doctor with?"

Ruben switched the umbrella from one hand to the other. "Remember that time Mr. Cobb followed us all the way from Camden Mercantile to the ferry just to give us that bag of corn seed we forgot?"

Daddy chuckled. "Thought he was gonna fall over dead the way his face was so red and he was breathing so hard." He winked at Ruben. "Looked just like a hog that's done ate too much."

"But he didn't have to come after us. He could have let us get all the way back home without that seed. Then we would've had to miss a whole 'nother day of work to fetch it."

Daddy cleared his throat. "You're right about that, son. It was mighty kind of Mr. Cobb to bring us that seed." Daddy gazed at the embers in the fireplace. "But there's something you got to always remember. Mr. Cobb's the boss man, and we ain't nothing but sharecroppers. Can't be bothering him with our troubles. Wouldn't want him thinking we can't do our work."

Ruben didn't have nothing to say to that. But I wasn't giving up. "Daddy," I said, "what if Aunt Doshie's wrong? What if the doctor knows something she don't?"

"Lu, I'm telling you, you got to put it out of your head. We're doing all we can do for your mama."

I felt heat rise into my cheeks. It wasn't true. We wasn't doing all we could do.

Just then Mama started coughing so hard she sat straight up in bed, knocking the umbrella from Ruben's hand. He scrambled to catch it while Daddy placed his hands on Mama's shoulders and eased her back down on the bed.

"It's okay," he said. "Everything's gonna be okay." Mama groaned, then rolled over and back again. Finally she settled on her side, and her breathing got quieter. Me and Daddy and Ruben looked at one another, our faces lit up with hope. Mama hadn't breathed that easy since before Rose was born. Maybe she was getting better now. Maybe that last mean cough was the one that turned the corner.

I stitched for a while longer as the rain kept coming down. Rose squirmed in her sleep, but settled right down when I patted her back. Soon my fingers got clumsy, so I tied off a knot and pushed my quilting things back into my pocket. Then I slid my eye patch under my pillow and closed my eyes. I started to say my prayers, but I reckon I was asleep before I even finished 'em.

The next morning, Daddy was already at the stove when I wiggled out from under the quilt so I could go to the outhouse. I don't reckon he got any sleep at all between caring for Mama and warming the milk so I could feed Rose.

Sure wasn't easy having a baby in the house. Or a sick mama.

Daddy stopped me before I got out the door of the cabin. "Lu," he said, "stay with your mama while I put on some water for grits."

I needed to get to that outhouse real bad, but I didn't want to cause no trouble with Daddy. So I just crossed my legs and nodded.

The rain had eased off to just a light drizzle, so wasn't no need for the umbrella no more. Rain still dripped from the ceiling and the room still had a foul smell, but I reckon I was getting used to it.

I smoothed the quilt under Mama's chin and made myself look at her hard. Her lips was blistered, and there was beads of sweat all around her hairline. And her eyes looked like they had sunk deeper into her head.

Was it just last night that I imagined she might be getting better? She sure didn't look no better right now.

"Found six eggs," Ruben said as he came through the front door. Soon as the door was shut, Mama jolted forward in another fit of coughing. I held her shoulders firm, same as I'd seen Daddy do. Soon as the coughing stopped, I eased her back down into the bed. When I pulled the quilt back up to her chin, I saw the one thing I was hoping I wouldn't.

"It's blood!" I said, lifting the quilt edge and fingering the damp spray of red spots. "She's coughing blood!" Wasn't no ignoring it this time. And wasn't no hiding it neither.

Daddy stopped his stirring and rushed over with the spoon still in his hand. He touched his finger to the blood, then lay his head on Mama's chest.

I had to turn away when Daddy's shoulders began to shake with sobs. I stood in front of the window and pushed the shutters open just a crack. The drizzle wet my face and fingers, but it didn't block the sound of Daddy's crying.

I looked for Delilah, but a mist hung in the air so thick I couldn't hardly see past the woodpile. The barn sat shapeless as a lump of lard and the Pettways' cabin was all but hidden. I'd lived in the same place my whole life, but right then everything about it seemed strange and unfamiliar. If it wasn't for the hens clucking from their hiding spots beneath the bushes, I'd swear it wasn't my home at all.

Dear Lord, thank you for the chickens. Bless 'em for giving eggs even in the rain.

I rested my elbows on the wet window frame and let the rain fall on my arms. What if I took them eggs to Camden and gave 'em to the doctor? Surely if I was offering payment, he wouldn't turn me away.

I pulled the shutters closed and joined Ruben at the table. "Ruben," I said, "wrap up them eggs."

Ruben rubbed the last egg clean and set it on the table. "What for?"

"I'm gonna go to Camden. To fetch Doc Nelson," I whispered so Daddy couldn't hear.

Ruben's eyes looked like they was gonna pop out of his head. "But you ain't never been there, Ludelphia. Besides, you ain't old enough to be going to Camden by yourself."

I swallowed. "You can't stop me."

Ruben was so quiet I wasn't sure if he'd heard what I said. Then he started shaking his head. "I should be the one to go, not you. I'm sixteen and you're only ten. I've been there before and you haven't."

"But you can't go, Ruben." I pushed my chin toward Daddy. "Look at him. He needs you for all the chores so he can be with Mama."

Ruben picked up one of the eggs and rolled it in his palm. "You heard what Daddy said, Ludelphia." Ruben wrapped his fingers around the egg and held it still. "Ain't nothing more to be done."

I bit down on my lip. Wasn't no time to cry. "Well, I'm not giving up." Not when this whole thing was all because of me. "I'm going to Camden," I said, crossing my arms against my chest. "Don't matter what you say."

Ruben stared at me for what seemed like forever. "Well, then," he said finally and began to bundle the eggs. "You take the ferry straight over. Willie Joe, he'll take care of you. Then don't you stop till you see the doctor's office."

Ruben looked back toward Daddy. "And whatever you do, you stay clear of Mrs. Cobb. You know, Mr. Cobb's wife?" Ruben leaned down till we was eye to eye. "You hear me, Lu? This family can't take nothing else bad happening. And last time we was in Camden, Mrs. Cobb had a mean look in her eye. Like a rattlesnake ready to strike."

I nodded. Mrs. Cobb didn't scare me near as much as it did seeing Mama lying helpless in the bed.

"Go on, now," he said. "Before Daddy hears us."

"You reckon he's gonna be mad?"

"Don't you worry none. I'll talk to him. Besides, you'll be back by suppertime. He won't hardly have time to miss you."

It was settled, then. I was gonna cross the river for the very first time.

Crossing the River

I RAN TO THE OUTHOUSE FIRST, THEN BACK ACROSS the front yard. The rain had slowed to a sprinkle, but there was still enough nip in the air to send a shiver down my arms. Mud squished between my toes as I got to the clothesline where Mama's apron sagged. Wasn't no time better than now for me to get that little piece of sash I needed for Mama's quilt.

I set the eggs down on the ground so I could reach up and pick loose the threads that connected the sash to the rest of the apron. Had to pull a little as I picked with my fingernail, to help loosen the seam. Didn't take but one good hard yank for it to come apart. As I stuffed the sash into my front pocket, I took off running for the footpath.

I stopped short when Delilah started braying. I couldn't just leave without giving her some breakfast.

I poured in an extra scoop on account of the rain and

gave her ears a scratch. "Don't you worry, Delilah. I'll be back before you know it." As I gave her one last pat on the neck, I caught a flash of yellow from the corner of my eye.

I looked the other way and started running.

I don't know why, but I didn't want Etta Mae to know I was going. I just wanted to do it. Then, when I had the doctor beside me, that's when I'd talk to Etta Mae.

I reckon I was afraid if I stopped moving I might start thinking about all the reasons it was crazy for me to go to Camden. If I didn't just keep putting one foot in front of the other, I might lose my courage.

As soon as I passed the footpath that led to Aunt Doshie's house, the rain stopped altogether. Up ahead I could see the whitewashed walls of Pleasant Grove Baptist Church. On the front steps I could just make out the tall thin shape of Reverend Irvin.

Of all days to be sneaking off from Gee's Bend, Sunday had to be the worst. Trouble was, the footpath went right in front of the church, so wasn't no avoiding Reverend Irvin.

I slowed to a walk and tried to think of what I might say to him. Soon as he spotted me, Reverend Irvin lifted his hand in a wave. "Morning, Ludelphia," he said. "You sure early this morning."

The less I said, the better, so I just waved. But wasn't no way I could get by without stopping. So soon as I got to the church steps, I gave him a smile. Would have been rude not to.

Reverend Irvin put his hands together like he was praying and pressed 'em against his mouth and nose. "Your mama doing any better today?"

"No, sir." I reached up to straighten my eye patch. "Reckon it's turned to pneumonia, like Aunt Doshie said." I hated saying them words. But better to focus on Mama than what I was doing out so early in the rain. "Now she's coughing up blood."

"Oh, Ludelphia." Reverend Irvin shook his head. "That why you came, then? To get me?"

I nodded, even though it wasn't why I came at all. It just sounded good. With Reverend Irvin praying over Mama here in Gee's Bend and me heading to Camden to get help, Mama just might make it. Besides, it wasn't a lie exactly. I just wasn't telling him everything I knew.

Reverend Irvin started down the church steps. "I'm sorry to hear it, Ludelphia. Ain't no finer lady than your mama. Not in Gee's Bend or anyplace."

I about cried when he said that. Because Reverend Irvin knew lots of folks. He'd been lots of places too. If he said my mama was a fine lady, then I knew it was really true.

"Run on, then," he said. "Tell your Daddy I'll be up there directly."

I nodded again. This time it felt like a lie through and through. Reckon Mama would wash my mouth out if she knew.

As Reverend Irvin went back into the church, I turned like I was heading down the footpath toward home. Wasn't right to fool him like this. But I could apologize later, after the doctor came and made Mama all better. By then it wouldn't matter much.

I waited a second more, then bolted into the woods so Reverend Irvin couldn't see me going in the other direction. He'd find out soon enough from Ruben and Daddy where I was.

By the time I got to the river, the sun was peeking through the clouds in places. But wasn't the sky that held my attention. It was the river.

The water was making some kind of racket, and it was flowing higher than I'd ever seen it. Why, it was a muddy mess, with all sorts of broken tree branches and dead leaves rushing past. I reckon it was on account of the storm, but that water was moving so fast the cable that held the ferry in place was groaning from the strain. I ain't never seen the river like that.

"Willie Joe! You there?" Usually he sat in a little lean-to that was built right on the bank of the river, and just as soon as anybody got close, he'd come out to greet them.

"Willie Joe?" I said again as I got closer to the lean-to. The door was open, but wasn't nobody inside. Wasn't no sound except the roar of the river.

Where was he? Wasn't a time I'd come down to the ferry when the ferry was there but Willie Joe wasn't.

"Willie Joe!" I hollered, throwing my head back. Up above, the clouds raced across the sky like they was in a contest with the river. They was in a hurry just like me.

I made another circle around the lean-to. Still no Willie Joe.

How on earth was I gonna get across now?

I sat myself on the wet riverbank to think a minute. If only Ruben was here. He'd know what to do. Or Etta Mae. I reckon she'd have some ideas.

What was it Mama always said? *It takes a heap of licks to strike a nail in the dark*. Wasn't no use wandering around aimlessly. I just needed to sit till I got a clear plan in my head. Then I could tackle that river.

Without even knowing it, I pulled my needle and cloth

out of my pocket. Put in a whole row of stitches before I even knew I was doing it.

When I was leaving, Ruben said for me to take the ferry straight over. Not to stop till I got to the doctor's office. Like it was all so simple. He didn't tell me nothing about what to do if Willie Joe wasn't around or if I couldn't find the doctor's office. Wasn't no map for me to look at and nobody for me to ask. All I had was my needle and some cloth and a bundle of six eggs.

I jerked my chin up and patted the ground all around me. What had I done with them eggs?

My face got hot with shame when I remembered I set them eggs down next to the clothesline. I'd run off without them.

Now how was I gonna pay Doc Nelson?

"Ain't no use thinking about that now," I said as I tucked away my stitching. Didn't make no difference about whether or not I had eggs if I didn't first get myself across that river.

I stood then and walked closer to the river's edge. Once I heard Teacher say the distance between Camden and Gee's Bend was the longest hundred yards he'd ever crossed. I reckon he should know, on account he used the ferry twice a day whenever he came to teach. But I can't say for sure because I ain't never measured it. To me it looked about as wide as the distance between the chinaberry tree in our front yard and the outhouse in back.

The ferry itself wasn't nothing more than logs tied together with rope. Most times it was for carrying folks to get their bags of seed and other things from Mr. Cobb at Camden Mercantile. But it was about as big as the inside of our cabin, so it could carry over a wagon and a pair of horses too.

I reckon it was the cables that made it strong. One cable held the ferry to a metal wheel way up high. The wheel ran along the other cable that was strung between two trees on either side of the river. So all Willie Joe had to do to get folks across was push his long pole against the bottom of the river. Then the little wheel would turn and the ferry would follow it straight across.

The pole. Wouldn't get nowhere unless I got hold of Willie Joe's pole.

I looked all along the riverbank till finally I found it hiding in some leaves that must have blown over it during the storm.

That pole was taller than I was. But once I got it firm in my hand, wasn't no more thinking about it. I held my breath and jumped from the bank to the ferry.

The logs dipped into the water when I landed, nearly

knocking me off balance. But I grabbed hold of the rail just in time.

I was on the river! For the first time in my whole life, there wasn't a bit of solid dirt under my feet. Just thousands of buckets of water.

I wished Mama could see me. Even if she was mad about it, I reckon she'd be proud too.

Above me the cable groaned as a tangle of tree branches slammed into the ferry. To keep myself from falling, I dug my toes in between the logs. I was working so hard to keep my feet in place, I forgot about my hands. Next thing I knew, Willie Joe's pole was rolling along the floor of the ferry.

As I scrambled after the pole, freezing water splashed onto my arms and legs. I gritted my teeth against the cold. Then, just as the pole was about to roll off the edge of the ferry, I got my fingers wrapped around it.

I grinned. Didn't matter that my dress was sticking to my legs and goose bumps was popping up all over. I was crossing the river!

Now was the time for the hard part. The ferry wobbled as I planted the pole into the muddy bottom of the river. I tried to do it just the way I'd seen Willie Joe do.

Trouble was, I wasn't as big as Willie Joe. And the current was so strong, it was like the ferry was stuck. It was acting all stubborn, the way Delilah does in the late afternoons after being in the field all day. The ferry just sat there straining to go downstream when I wanted it to go across.

I threw all my weight against the pole. I pushed so hard the muscles in my arms burned.

"You can do it," I said as I planted the pole again, this time in front of the ferry. As the logs shifted underneath me and we began to inch along, I knew it was working. The ferry was moving!

Again and again I lifted the pole and planted it into the mud at the bottom of the river. Again and again the ferry moved a little closer to the other shore.

"Dear Lord, thank you!" I said to the sky as the wheel kept on turning. Then I thought of Etta Mae. She was gonna love this story. Silly old eye patch couldn't stop me.

By the time I got to the center of the river, my breath came out in quick puffs and it felt like my arms was on fire. Wasn't no time to stop, though. Not with the water rushing along and the ferry bucking like a mule that ain't been broke.

I lifted the pole again and pushed it deep in the water. This time the pole went down and down and down without stopping. Wasn't no bottom in this part of the river!

And the current was so strong it was sucking the pole right out of my fingers.

I gasped as the pole slipped into the water and disappeared for a moment, then popped back up to the surface. I reached, but it was already on its way down the river. It got smaller and smaller till I couldn't see it no more.

What was I gonna do now? Wasn't no way to get the ferry across the river without a pole, unless you counted swimming. Which I didn't, on account I ain't never learned how.

Mama, why didn't you let Daddy or Ruben teach me to swim? Just because I got this old eye patch. Ain't no reason for not learning to do outside things.

Just then a gust of wind caught the ferry. The cable that held the ferry to the wheel screeched like a hungry owl. The cable began to unravel, slowly at first, then faster and faster. Then I heard a popping sound and the ferry jerked free. Next thing I knew, me and the ferry wasn't going across no more. We was heading downstream same as Willie Joe's pole.

I got low as I could to the bottom of the ferry. I mean, we was flying down that river. I ain't never gone so fast in my life. Freezing cold water was rushing into my face, pushing against my eye patch. I couldn't catch my breath, and I thought I was gonna die for sure.

Where in the world did this river go? I tried to picture the map Teacher showed us at school. I knew the river looped and turned all through Alabama, and at the end it dumped into Mobile Bay. Wasn't no telling where I'd end up.

I looked behind me. How far was I now from Gee's Bend? How far from Camden?

Wasn't nothing I could see that looked familiar to me. I reckon I thought the river would look the same no matter where you was. But I got to tell you, that river was full of surprises. Wasn't long before it got wider, like it was turning into a lake. And the water started to slow down. Didn't help me none. I still couldn't swim and now I was a whole lot farther from the shore.

What would happen if I jumped? Would I sink under the water and never come back up? Mama always said it's best not to rush into things. That sometimes the answer to a problem will come to you if you just wait it out.

But what did Mama know about this river? She was born in Gee's Bend and ain't never spent a night noplace else. Only time she ever crossed over was when the blackberries was ripe and ready to sell.

She was scared of the river, that's what I think. Her mama never did teach her how to swim neither.

Well, I didn't have time for being scared. Wasn't all

that far to the shore. Couldn't be no farther than the distance from the chinaberry tree to the last cabin on our row. And could be my arms and legs would get in there and know just what to do.

I checked my pocket to be sure my needle and cloth was shoved in just as far as they could go. Then I got real close to the edge of the ferry, sucked in my breath, and did the only thing I could think of.

I jumped.

I mean to tell you, that water didn't have no manners whatsoever. Didn't stop to say hello or how do you do. It was like a door that was open one second, slammed shut the next.

At first I just let myself sink. My ears popped as I drifted down, and when I opened my eye all I could see was a billion bubbles.

Wasn't the worst thing in the world being all covered up with water. It was cold but heavy. Like being in bed with three quilts covering me from head to toe. I liked the way my arms and legs was floating like they didn't have no weight to 'em at all.

Trouble was, my head wasn't popping up to the top the way a piece of cork does on a fishing line. I didn't have no idea what to do.

Just then my chest started to ache on the inside. I

reckon that's what made my legs start kicking and my arms start waving.

Slowly my body began to rise toward daylight. I kicked harder as the water seemed to get thinner, and my dress started to float up around my middle. Just when I thought my chest was gonna explode, my head popped out of the water and my mouth opened wide so I could drag in some fresh air.

I pushed my shoulders back and lifted my chin above the water. The ferry was getting smaller and smaller as it kept on going down the river. Was Willie Joe ever gonna be mad at me when he found out about the ferry getting loose and floating away!

But wasn't no use in thinking about that. My legs was getting real tired, like they wasn't gonna go much longer. I pointed myself toward the riverbank and paddled with my arms as fast as they would go.

Little by little, I moved toward the shore. Wasn't much farther to go now. Just had to keep my arms and legs moving a little while longer.

In front of me a fallen tree stretched out from the riverbank like an arm reaching to catch me. If I could just get to that tree! Then I could pull myself out of the cold water that was making my muscles burn and my skin shiver.

I gave two more powerful kicks and stretched my fingers as far as they could go. But before I could grab hold of the fallen tree, the water started pulling me under. It was like two giant hands latched onto my legs and yanked me down under that tree.

I sputtered as my mouth went underwater before I was ready. I was so close to the shore. Why couldn't I get out of the water?

My mind went dark except for Mama's face. My legs pumped hard against the current. The river wanted to pull me under, but I wouldn't let it. I was gonna get to Camden. I was gonna find Doc Nelson, and he was gonna save Mama's life. Wasn't nothing gonna stop me from getting to the other side.

I CAN'T SAY HOW IT HAPPENED, BUT NEXT THING I knew I had my arms wrapped around a tree trunk, and arm over arm I was hauling myself up. As soon as I felt solid ground under my feet, I fell in a heap same way Mama did the day Rose was born. My heart was thumping like it was gonna come right out of my chest, and I was shaking so bad I wasn't sure I would ever stop. And wasn't no telling where I was.

But none of that mattered. What mattered was that I was alive, and I had crossed over to the other side.

I don't know how long it was I stayed in that same spot. When I rolled over from my belly to my back, the sun was high and the clouds had all disappeared.

Where in the world was I? I sat in a little patch of light, but all I could see around me was pine trees. Pine trees that looked just like the ones in Gee's Bend. Except I knew they wasn't.

I eased up to a sitting position and smoothed my hands across the front of my dress. The sun felt warm on my back, but my whole dress was soaked through and sticking to my skin. The front was streaked with orange mud, and the seam of my pocket was torn. Ain't no amount of scrubbing that'll get them orange stains out. But miracle of miracles, my needle and scraps of cloth was still there.

Mama, if this here needle can make it across the Alabama River, you can make it too. You can stop coughing and get out of that bed and get back to stitching quilts in the evenings.

I squeezed the water from the cloth pieces and spread them out on the sunny patch of pine straw to dry. I held the needle between my finger and thumb, gentle enough so as not to draw blood. Such a tiny little thing. But just the touch of it made me feel better. Like right between my fingers I was holding a piece of home.

I reckon it just takes a bit of time for the water to all the way drain out of your ears before your mind can start working straight again. Or could be I was just so glad to be out of that river I wasn't thinking no more about what a hurry I was in. Because instead of jumping up and running my way back the direction I came from, I took the wet thread and put it right through the needle. Didn't even have to lick it.

Then I knotted the thread with my fingers and moved the needle in and out of them calico pieces from Mama's apron. They was looking good in my quilt, just like I thought they would.

I'd need a plain piece of cloth next. Some solid color to set off the calico. Because my mama didn't like no busy quilt. She liked there to be order enough to it so it didn't hurt your eyes when you looked at it.

That's when I remembered my torn pocket. I set the cloth I was working onto the ground beside me and started picking at the seam with my fingers. Had to be real careful not to rip a hole in the dress. I sure didn't want to waste no thread patching a silly old hole.

Soon as the pocket was free, I held it up against the work I'd already done. Perfect! Wouldn't take me long to stitch it in, neither. Soon as I was done, I'd be on my way.

What was Mama doing this very second? Was she having one of them coughing spells? What about baby Rose and Etta Mae? Had Ruben told any of 'em yet about me going to Camden?

I sat there stitching and thinking till the sun was

straight up in the sky. My dress was starting to dry and I didn't feel nearly so waterlogged as I had before. I rolled my head from side to side to loosen my neck, then I smoothed the quilt against my legs, checking each seam. The quilt was big enough now to cover my lap, like a real colorful napkin. I know Mama would be proud of how fast I was getting it done.

Would Mama like the colors I picked? I tucked the needle into a tight seam and held the quilt up in the air to get a look from a different angle. Would she be mad about me taking them pieces from her apron? I turned the quilt in the air, looking at it this way and that. Soon I would run out of thread. Wasn't but a few inches hanging down like the tail of a kite.

I lay back in the grass, the sun warm on my face. I closed my eyes and got a picture of Rose in my mind. Rose when she was brand-new, before I knew how bad things was with Mama.

My eyelids got heavy and my breathing got regular. Just one more minute, I thought, just need to rest one more minute, then I'll start walking back toward Camden.

One minute turned to two. Two minutes turned to three. After not sleeping none the whole night and then fighting the river, I reckon my body couldn't handle it no more.

While Mama lay there coughing and shaking, I slept. I slept like a baby. I slept like Rose.

It was a squirrel that woke me. A little bush-tailed squirrel rooting around in the straw for stray nuts to stuff in its mouth and carry home to its nest.

I saw the squirrel first, then the sun. It was starting to come down already, and I knew what that meant. Wasn't much daylight left.

I jerked up, smacking my tongue against the roof of my mouth. It was dry and pasty-feeling, like biscuits before you bake 'em.

I scrambled to my feet. How could I have fallen to sleep? Etta Mae wouldn't have done that. Or Ruben. I reckon if one of them had come with me, I'd be in Camden already.

I smoothed down my dress. It was wrinkled now, but at least it was nearly dry. If only my legs didn't feel so wobbly. It was like my mind was awake but the rest of me was still trying to catch up.

I scooped up my quilting things and ground my teeth together as the muscles in my back and legs complained. Wasn't no time for that now. Not with night coming on so fast.

Why did the days have to be so short in November?

And me so far down the river. Was it five miles? Ten? The way the river moved, I just couldn't be sure. The only thing certain was that there wasn't no way I was gonna get back to Gee's Bend by nightfall. No way at all.

I pushed air out through my nose the way Delilah does when she's looking for more feed but there ain't none in the bucket.

Could I even get to Camden before nightfall? I rubbed my hands against my bare arms. I sure didn't want to sleep the night on the riverbank the way Etta Mae did. Not with that cool breeze blowing.

Beside me the river flowed with no worries whatsoever. Just moseyed right along.

That's when it came to me. If I just stayed close to the river, I'd wind up where I was supposed to be. All I had to do was walk back the way I'd come and I would find Camden. I would find Camden and get Doc Nelson and then I'd bring him back to Gee's Bend to help Mama.

Wasn't nothing else for me to do except put one foot in front of the other. I reckon I walked five or six miles, right along the river. Didn't take all that long because I was used to walking. On account there wasn't a single motorcar in Gee's Bend. We'd hitch Delilah up to a wagon sometimes, but that was for hauling cotton mostly. Not for folks to ride in.

The pine trees swayed above me as night moved in and the air got cooler. My nose and ears was so cold, I knew they'd start going numb if I didn't find cover soon. Wasn't nothing but trees far as I could see. But I knew from living in Gee's Bend that the trees had to stop someplace. I just had to keep going and then there would be a cotton field or maybe a row of cabins.

Whatever energy I'd gotten from sleeping soon disappeared and was replaced by a gnawing in my belly. After all I'd been through that day, I needed food. Hadn't had a bite to eat since breakfast.

First I tried to forget about it by running. Trouble was, running made my knees and shoulders ache. After just a few minutes, my whole body was complaining. You'd think I was falling to pieces. Didn't help none that I was alone in a place I ain't never been before.

I kicked through a pile of leaves. Looked like hickory, the way they was half yellow, half brown. I bet they was real pretty in sunlight. Wasn't no pine trees alongside this part of the river. Just oak and hickory and elm, their branches nearly bare of leaves. Wouldn't Daddy love to have some of that wood to put on the fire. I bet it'd last all night long.

Goose bumps popped up on my arms. What I wouldn't give to be in front of a fire right now. Or under a quilt.

That's when I remembered the quilt in my hands. I real quick unfolded it and rubbed it against my arms. Right away them goose bumps disappeared.

Mama, are you getting any better? Or just worse? All day I've been working to get some help for you. I wish I'd done better. I wish I could just snap my fingers and things would be just the way I want them to be.

I crossed my arms against my chest. I had to get to Doc Nelson. I had to get Mama some help before it was too late.

I had other worries too. What if Daddy was mad about me going to Camden? What if he was mad at Ruben? I sure didn't want Ruben to get in no trouble. And what about the ferry? Folks in Gee's Bend wouldn't have no idea what happened to it. Or to me.

What if they was all worried about me? What if I never did make it to Camden and never made it home neither? What if I died, and Mama died, and Daddy had to raise Rose all alone?

A chill came across me, but I couldn't hardly shiver, my arms and legs was so worn out. Seemed like even the calluses on my feet was aching. All of a sudden a picture came in my head of them high-heeled shoes. They might be hard to walk in to start with, but I reckon they'd keep all them little acorns from digging into my feet. My belly grumbled, and I knew I wasn't gonna be able to go on much longer.

Next time I looked up at the sky, the sun was nearly gone. An owl called, and another one answered. I felt my belly sink about as low as it could get.

Then in the far-off distance I saw a light. It flashed, then was gone.

Was it lightning? Please, Lord, don't let it be lightning. Don't need another storm.

When the flash turned into a steady light, I knew it wasn't no storm.

I reckon that's when I forgot all about my plan to follow the river. Because soon as I saw that light shining like that, I turned and started walking toward it.

Wasn't too long before the forest thinned out and I could see the stubble of a cotton field that had already been picked clean. As I eased into a run, all my aches and pains, the hunger, the tight muscles, all of it was forgotten. The cool air that had once made me shiver now made me feel like I was more alive than ever. My mind seemed clear and nimble as I made my way through the cotton field. Not once did my sore feet come down on one of them sharp cotton stalks.

By the time I was halfway across, I could tell where

the light was coming from. It was a metal gate shining silver in the setting sun. Attached to the gate was a fence.

I grinned and wiped the sweat from my forehead with a corner of the quilt. Where there was a fence, there was cows. And where there was cows, someplace close by there had to be a barn.

Mrs. Cobb

WHEN I GOT TO THE GATE, I COULDN'T BELIEVE
how wide it was. I reckon when it was opened it was big
enough to drive two wagons through, side by side. But it
was shut tight and locked with a chain and padlock.

The fence turned out to be four lines of barbed wire.
The wire was tight and not a bit rusty, and the wood
posts was free of rot. Wasn't no way I could stretch those
wires enough to slip through, and it was too tall for me
to get over. I only had one choice, and that was to crawl
underneath.

Careful to keep my head below the wire, I lay on my
belly and pushed off with my toes. I half slid, half wiggled,
pushing the quilt forward with one hand and grabbing
tufts of pasture grass with the other. Didn't want them
barbs snagging my hair or dress. No telling how long it
might take me to get untangled.

Soon as I was all clear, I dusted myself off and set off walking again.

My legs wobbled as I dodged cow patties. I listened for the river, but I couldn't hear it no more.

Instead I heard purple martins calling to each other as they got their last meal of the day. I heard crickets chirping and field mice just starting to rustle around in the tall grass. Someplace close by, cows was lowing, but I couldn't see 'em. And from someplace else there was the clang of a dinner bell.

The sun was gone now and the first stars was peeking out of the darkening sky. In the distance I could see the pasture was broken by a patch of trees. Next to the trees was two houses. One had a rusted metal roof, the other looked to be shingled. I ain't never seen houses so big, but I didn't need nobody to tell me which one was for folks to live in and which one was the barn. My nose would tell me the difference.

Sure enough, once I got close, I could smell hay and manure. The animals was already shut up for the night, but they was still making small grunts and bleats as they settled down to sleep.

"Hello," I called softly, just outside the tall wood doors. Wasn't likely I'd get a reply, but it didn't seem right just walking into a barn that didn't belong to me.

When nobody answered, I lifted the rusty latch and eased inside the door. The big door squealed on its hinges, and from someplace in the darkness a cat called.

The barn smelled just like home, but it wasn't. It belonged to somebody else, and I had no business being in it.

Should I go up to the house and let them folks know I'm here? Should I just go on up and knock on their door? If Mama ever told me what was the polite thing to do, I sure couldn't remember. Wasn't like we had farms like this in Gee's Bend.

I sighed and sank into a mound of hay some goats was chewing on. "It's just for one night," I said aloud. What else could I do? I was worn out from the river and all that walking. I needed rest, and I didn't have no idea where I was. I couldn't go banging on somebody's door after it was already dark. No telling what they might do.

No, I'd just have to wait till morning. I'd get up before dawn and scoot out of the barn, and nobody would even know I had been someplace I wasn't supposed to be.

I picked up a long stalk of hay and put the tip in my mouth. Tasted like alfalfa. My insides jumped in excitement. Delilah would be jealous if she knew.

I kept chewing the end of the alfalfa till my belly

quieted. Beside me a tall black mare nickered and rested her nose on the top of my head. I reached up so she could smell my palm, then leaned my head against the hard wood of the horse's stall.

The mare's nose was smoother than Delilah's. And the skin around her mouth was silky as Rose's cheek.

Was Delilah missing me yet? What about Daddy? By now he'd know I wasn't coming home.

I settled deeper into the pile and pulled off my eye patch so I could tuck it under the quilt top I was using for a pillow. As I closed my eyes, I got a picture of Daddy and Ruben beside Mama's bed.

Dear Lord, please don't let them be too worried about me. Let Mama's breath come easy and give baby Rose sweet dreams. Just a few more hours now. Then tomorrow, get me to Camden so I can find Doc Nelson and bring him home to Gee's Bend.

This time it wasn't a squirrel but the crowing of a rooster that woke me. Don't reckon nobody could sleep through that sound.

At first I didn't know where I was. But soon as I unfolded my legs and tried to stand up, I remembered. My whole body hurt, worse even than the time Delilah was in a mood and her hooves caught me right in the belly. And my eye itched. The one that don't work no more. But I put the eye patch in place anyhow. Just for Mama.

Outside the door I heard whistling. The human kind. And it was getting closer.

I backed myself toward the wall of the mare's stall, hoping it would hide me. But before I could get there, my heel turned the wrong way.

"Ow," I said as I landed on my backside. Well, I'd done it now. Wasn't no way for me to hide after all that racket.

Sure enough, the whistling stopped. I froze the way a rabbit does when it smells a dog. Then the door swung wide, creaking like a chorus of frogs.

At first I couldn't see nothing but sunlight. I put my arm over my head to shield my eye and waited for the world to come into focus.

"Lookie what the storm blew in." It was a lady's voice, but it had a rough edge to it. Soon as I could make her out, my mouth dropped open.

She was white. That was the biggest thing. My whole life I ain't never met nobody except colored folks like me. She was so pale it was like she wasn't even alive. I wanted to reach out and touch her cheek, just to prove she was real.

She had her hair all piled up on the top of her head and held in place with shiny pins. From the waist up, she looked just like one of them ladies in the newspaper ad. From the waist down was a whole other story. She had big black boots peeking from below the hem of her dress. And hiding there in the folds of her blue calico skirt was the barrel of a shotgun.

I pushed my feet into the packed dirt floor, flattening my back against the horse stall. What was she doing with a shotgun?

Then it hit me.

There I was, a stranger in her barn. A little black girl with a patch over one eye.

My heart raced and I could feel sweat prickling my brow. She had every right to shoot me.

The lady pressed the shotgun into the floor and leaned on it like it was a cane. Then she twisted toward the barn door. "Patrick!" she said, throwing her head back. "It's not an armadillo." She chuckled and flashed a big toothy grin.

"No?" Patrick said, poking his head into the barn, his lips puckered. "Figured the way the yard's all tore up, it had to be an armadillo. Them critters been known to dig runs up to twenty-five feet long."

His eyes got wide soon as he saw me. "Well, I'll be. You

was right on the money, Mrs. Cobb. Should've knowed you was."

Patrick squatted down next to me. He looked just like Reverend Irvin, only his hair was white and he had a beard. My shoulders relaxed a little seeing such a familiar-looking face.

"Child, how'd you end up in this here barn?" Patrick said. Then he lowered his voice, like he was telling me a secret. "Ain't been thieving, now, have you?"

"Nossir, no'm." I shook my head and looked from one to the other. "Ain't nothing like that. It's just my mama's real sick so I'm on my way to Camden to fetch Doc Nelson."

Mrs. Cobb moved in closer. She poked around my legs with the barrel of the shotgun. Like she was looking for something. "That true? Now, you wouldn't be telling me a story, would you, girl?"

"No'm." I hunched my shoulders and tried to keep my lips from trembling. "I promise it ain't like that. I just fell to sleep here. The ferry busted loose and took me down the river. I walked fast as I could, but this is as far as I got before it turned dark." I stopped to catch my breath. "I didn't mean no harm. It's just I ain't never been to Camden before." I blinked back tears. "I don't even know where I am!"

LEAVING GEE'S BEND

They was both silent as I straightened my eye patch. Mrs. Cobb looked at Patrick, then back at me. There was something in that look made me want to get up and run. But where in the world was I gonna go?

"Girl, did you say you rode the ferry?" Mrs. Cobb's voice was softer now, gentle even. Her lips was curved into a half smile that didn't all the way reach her eyes.

"You from Gee's Bend, then?" she said, tracing the curve of my chin with her fingernail.

I wanted to give her the right answer, the one Mama would say. But I couldn't think what that was. So I just nodded.

"Well, that changes everything." Mrs. Cobb glanced back at the old man. "Remember, Patrick? It was Mr. Cobb himself who told me 'take care of the folks in Gee's Bend.'"

"Yes'm." Patrick reached around the side of the door. "Want me to hitch up the wagon?"

I looked from one to the other. What was they talking about, take care of the folks in Gee's Bend? Was they planning to help us? Lord knows, times had been hard lately with the cotton crop coming in so small. Wasn't no place for us to go except farther and farther in debt.

Mrs. Cobb put her finger to her lip like she was thinking. Then her face lightened up. "Oh, no, Patrick. This young lady came all the way from Gee's Bend. Poor thing spent the whole night in the barn." Her fingers drummed on my shoulder. "Crank up the motorcar."

A motorcar? I was gonna ride in a motorcar? Fast as they go, I'd have the doctor at Mama's bedside by suppertime. Mrs. Cobb sure was the answer to my prayers.

"You gonna take me to Camden?"

"That's right." Mrs. Cobb ground her teeth together hard enough so that I could hear 'em.

Then I remembered. Mrs. Cobb! The one Ruben had warned me about. Surely he wasn't talking about *this* Mrs. Cobb.

I looked up at her long neck and straight back. She caught me looking and flashed me another smile.

"But first," she said, her hand now on my shoulder, "first, I'm taking our special guest up to the big house. So we can have us a private conversation."

She was treating me so nice, like I was kinfolk or something. Had to be another Mrs. Cobb, that's all there was to it. Ruben couldn't be talking about this one.

"Come on, then," Mrs. Cobb said, motioning with the shotgun. I real quick grabbed my quilting things. As I checked to be sure my needle was in place, something moved between my legs. I could hear its little clawed feet clicking against the hard floor.

"It's that stinking armadillo!" Mrs. Cobb screamed. Like the world was coming to an end.

Right away Patrick scrambled after it. But that armadillo was faster than he was.

"Hold on, Patrick," Mrs. Cobb said, lifting that shotgun. Just about before I could blink she had cocked and aimed and was ready to shoot.

The quilt dropped to the ground as I plugged my ears with my fingers and squeezed shut my eyes.

Next thing I saw was that armadillo lying on its side, a hole right through its thick skin.

I ran over to where Patrick was kneeling beside the little body. Its insides was blasted out. I reckon it was a good thing I didn't have nothing more than alfalfa hay in my belly right then. Otherwise there might have been another mess to clean up.

Now, why did Mrs. Cobb have to do that? Why did she have to go and shoot that poor armadillo? I swiped my eyes. Mama would have got me to chase it out into the woods, maybe to the swamp even. Wouldn't have been no bother to nobody then.

"Reckon I'll dig a hole for it," Patrick said.

"Not now, Patrick," Mrs. Cobb said sharply. "Go on now and crank the motorcar."

Patrick whispered something that sounded like a

prayer. Then he turned away from the armadillo, his brow creased and mouth turning down at the corners.

It wasn't just me. Patrick didn't think it was right neither.

I took a quick glance back at Mrs. Cobb. She was holding herself tall and stiff, her face blank as a cotton field that's ready for seed. "Hurry up, now," she said.

Wasn't nothing else for me to do but pick up my quilting things and head toward the door. Mrs. Cobb fell in step behind me. After just two steps, something poked me in the center of my back. I wasn't sure if it was her fingers or the barrel of that shotgun, but I didn't dare turn around to find out.

The Big House

THE BIG HOUSE WAS PAINTED WHITE, AND THE ROOF had green shingles. There was a porch winding all the way around it, and below the porch was yellow mums and purple pansies growing in the cleanest beds you ever did see. Not a weed in sight.

Was this the kind of house Etta Mae lived in when she was working in Mobile? Why, there was even a rail to hold on to when you climbed the stairs. And the front door had real glass panes.

Mrs. Cobb held the door open so I could walk right through. She leaned the shotgun against the wall next to the front door. "Welcome to our home," she said with a small bow, like I was a queen or something. Then she held out her hand. "My name is Mrs. Cobb. And you are?"

"Ludelphia. Ludelphia Bennett," I said, giving a curtsy just the way Mama taught me. She pulled back a little, her eyes looking me up and down. Then she wrinkled her nose. I reckon I looked a sight after dragging myself through the river and the woods and sleeping in the barn.

"Let's get you cleaned up, Ludelphia Bennett," she said. "Washroom's right down the hall."

A washroom too? Ain't never washed myself in nothing but the spring or a metal tub set out on the front porch of the cabin. I couldn't wait to see what it looked like.

Mrs. Cobb stepped back as I hurried across the shiny wood floor and set my feet on a rug that stretched down the hallway. You ain't never stepped on a rug so soft. My feet seemed to sink and kept sinking right deep down into it.

"It's like fresh pulled cotton, only it don't puff up into the air," I said, looking back at Mrs. Cobb. Her eyes was cast down and her face was frozen.

What was the matter now? Had I said something wrong?

Soon as I looked down, I knew. It was my dirty feet. They had left footprints all along that fluffy rug.

"I'm sorry." I bent down to wipe 'em away.

She waved me away with her hand, then reached up to tuck a stray hair behind her ear. "Go on to the washroom."

The hallway to the washroom seemed to go on forever. It was wide, almost like a room itself, and there was no newspaper on the walls and no cracks noplace. Instead there was pictures covered in glass and hung in silver frames. All the way down the hall they went, making one long row. I stopped in the middle of the hallway where there was one of Mrs. Cobb in a long white dress holding a bunch of flowers. Another one had a baby girl sitting all proper-like on Mrs. Cobb's knees.

I held my quilt with one hand and reached toward the picture with the other. I ain't never seen pictures of real people before. Even the ones in the newspaper was just drawings. And there was something about the baby that made me want to get real close.

"I wouldn't do that if I was you." I pulled back my hand and faced Patrick.

When I opened my mouth to speak, he put his finger to his lips. "Shhhh, quiet now."

I wanted to ask him about Mrs. Cobb and the armadillo. I wanted to know if she was the Mrs. Cobb Ruben warned me about. But Patrick didn't give me no time to say any of them things. "It true you from Gee's Bend?"

"Yessir." I looked from Patrick's face back down the hallway. I could just see the doorway to what must be the washroom.

"You not one of them witches, is you? The witches of Gee's Bend?"

I wrinkled my brow. Witches? My mind went right to Etta Mae and the devil's lye and the knife she shoved into Mama's mattress.

Witches of Gee's Bend. The way he said it was like something everybody knew about, like "Montgomery is the capital of Alabama." And witch*es*, as in more than one. What on earth was he talking about?

I gripped the quilt top that was still in my hand. "Nossir." Wasn't nothing I could say for sure about witches.

Patrick held my gaze. "I reckon you'd be better off if you was."

I couldn't get a breath. "Better off?" What did he mean?

"Look, child. Mrs. Cobb done had her some hard times lately. Her mind ain't quite right. Unless you got some magical powers, best thing for you to do is get yourself back to Gee's Bend just as soon as you can." Patrick's eyes got a little shiny then. "I'd help you if I could. But times is hard. I got to have this work. Got seven children to feed."

It was too much. Witches and Mrs. Cobb and Patrick and seven children. I couldn't sort it all out right then.

As Patrick tiptoed away from me down the hall, I

hurried into the washroom and closed the door behind me. I still didn't know what, or who, Patrick was talking about. Wasn't nothing magical about me, that's for sure. Or else I would have done healed Mama all by myself.

But what if what Patrick was talking about was the same bad luck stuff Daddy talked about? Or the bad things Etta Mae said happened in Mobile.

Dear Lord. What if the witch was me? What if the reason Mama got sick was all because of me?

I stood in front of the sink that looked like a fancy bowl. Then I turned the handle that was shaped like an X. No toting water up from the spring in this house. It poured into the sink just like a little waterfall.

And above the sink I saw something I ain't never seen before, at least not clear and close up the way it was now. My own face looking back at me.

Was I ever a mess! No wonder Mrs. Cobb was poking at me with her shotgun. Bits of hair was fuzzing up all around my braids, and even with my dark skin you could tell my cheeks was all smudged up with dirt and Lord knows what else. And the eye patch. Can't forget that. It was tattered around the edges, I reckon from pushing it on and off all the time.

Was this what a witch looked like? A witch from Gee's Bend?

I lifted the eye patch. Surely a witch wouldn't have an eye that was useless as mine.

Wasn't no answers in that mirror. None whatsoever. "Oh, Mama." I snapped the eye patch back in place and washed up quick as I could. Before I opened the door I was careful to wipe down the sink with the small towel that was hanging from a silver hook next to the mirror. Didn't want to make more work for Mrs. Cobb. Not when she was gonna take me to Camden in a motorcar.

"Mrs. Cobb?" I said as I came out of the washroom. She was waiting by the front door, right where I left her.

"This way, Ludelphia. Come have yourself a seat in the living room while Adelaide fixes you some breakfast. Can't be running off to Camden without a nice breakfast, now can we?"

My belly starting rumbling just from the talk of breakfast. If I'd known how nice Mrs. Cobb was, I would have knocked on the door the night before. Wouldn't have had to sleep the whole night in the barn.

We came into the living room by walking under a doorway that had an arch in it. There was a fireplace with a fancy mantel clock, and the facing wall was all windows that looked out over a pasture that was dotted with cows. In the middle of the room was a giant piano. Not box-shaped like we had in church, but real big and rounded on one side. It was shiny black and it gleamed like it'd been polished just that morning.

"Do you play?" I said as I walked toward it. If Etta Mae was here, she'd make the whole house lift off the ground with the sound of her playing.

"Of course," Mrs. Cobb said. Of course. I nearly bit my tongue for asking such a silly question. Why else would she have a piano?

Mrs. Cobb walked toward the piano. She ran her finger along the shiny black top of the piano as she came around the other side. "Would you like me to play something for you?"

I clapped my hands together. "Do you know 'Swing Low, Sweet Chariot'? That's my favorite. Ain't heard nobody play it ever since they sold the church piano. Why, I'd just about die to hear that song, Mrs. Cobb!"

"Never heard of that one," Mrs. Cobb said, her face flat. "But what about this one?" Mrs. Cobb arched her fingers over the keys and began to play. It was a happy tune, like something you'd dance to. Not like "Swing Low, Sweet Chariot" at all.

"'The Entertainer.' By Scott Joplin," she said when she was done. Then she got a far-off look in her eye. "My niece, Sarah . . . she'd dance around every time I played that one. Her little eyes just sparkled."

"Yes'm," I said. "It's a right good song. But 'Swing Low, Sweet Chariot' is still my favorite."

Mrs. Cobb gave me a look like I'd hurt her, and I knew I'd gone and said the wrong thing. "Well, pardon me," she said, putting her white hand against her throat. Then she banged out a few awful-sounding chords that didn't sound anything at all like "The Entertainer."

For a minute it seemed like Mrs. Cobb had forgotten all about me. Then she real quick lifted herself from the piano bench and scooped up her shotgun.

"Adelaide! Got some breakfast ready for our guest?"

"Yes'm," a sweet voice called. "It's waiting in the dining room."

Mrs. Cobb waved her hand in the direction of the archway. "Shall we?"

I followed Mrs. Cobb into a room that had a long table topped with a lace cloth. There was china dishes laid out for a dozen folks. My mouth watered thinking about all the food that would fit on them plates. And on each plate except one was a white napkin folded so it looked like a bird that was ready to start flying.

I ain't never seen nothing so fancy. Why, if I had just one of them napkins I could add a whole other section to my quilt. Wouldn't Mama be tickled about that?

Wasn't no mystery where I was supposed to sit. It was

the only plate that had steam curling up from it. There was a fluffy white biscuit and two kinds of preserves to choose from. There was sausage links fat as three fingers. And not grits, but hash-browned potatoes.

I sure was in for a treat. I couldn't hardly stop myself from scooping everything up with my fingers. But one look at Mrs. Cobb and I knew I'd best use the fork and knife.

Just as I was spreading fig preserves onto my biscuit, Mrs. Cobb set a bottle on the table. I didn't have no idea where it came from, but I knew just what it was.

It was a Coke to drink. A genuine Coca-Cola. I ain't never had one of 'em before, just seen 'em in the newspaper pages. Wasn't no money for things like that. Nothing but the essentials, Mama always said.

"For me?" I said. A Coke for breakfast? I'd always imagined it as a treat for a blistering-hot afternoon, not first thing in the morning. Who ever heard of such a thing?

"Of course." She watched me closely as I reached for it. The bottle felt cool and wet under my fingers, like it was sweating. Dear Lord, what if it slipped through my hands and spilled? I put my other hand up under the bottle to make sure that didn't happen.

"Go on," Mrs. Cobb said, leaning back in her chair.

I real slow lifted the bottle and put it to my lips. It'd been a whole day since I'd had something to eat or drink! Unless you counted river water and alfalfa.

I closed my eyes and took a small sip. It was good and cold. Mrs. Cobb must have stored it outside all night long to get it that cold. And it bubbled as it went down, like I was swallowing a bunch of air. I wrinkled my nose and Mrs. Cobb laughed. It was an honest laugh, one that came from someplace deep inside her belly. But soon as she heard herself, it changed to a hollow sound.

"Now, when you get home, Ludelphia, I want you to tell everybody Mrs. Cobb gave you a Coke. Ice-cold sunshine. Just like the label says. You see what they say about that."

"Yes'm," I said. Then I did something I knew I shouldn't. "Mrs. Cobb?" I said. "You reckon I could have one of them napkins for this here quilt?" I held up the bundle. "I'm making it for my mama."

Things got so quiet I could hear the mantel clock ticking from the other room. I was sure I had gone and said the very wrong thing. Again. Mama would die of embarrassment if she knew.

Just when I was fixing to tell Mrs. Cobb I was sorry for being so rude, she pulled one of them napkins from its spot and real quick snapped it in the air so that the fancy folds fell out of it. Wasn't a bird no more, just a square of cloth.

"It's yours," she said, dropping the napkin into my lap.

I don't reckon she would've given me that napkin if she was mad. She looked from me to the plate, like what she wanted was for me to eat. So I ate bite after bite and washed it all down with that Coke. I couldn't remember a time when I had so much for breakfast. But before I could get the words "thank you" out of my mouth, there came a buzzing sound from outside. Like a giant bumblebee. I ain't never heard a sound like that before in my life.

Mrs. Cobb stood up. "You ready to go to Camden?"

"Yes'm," I said, placing the empty bottle on the table. Then I followed Mrs. Cobb to the front door.

As I walked out, I glanced back at the smooth walls and the pictures that hung in the hallway. I wanted to remember everything so I could tell Mama. When my eye drifted down and found the rug again, I saw that my foot-prints was gone. That rug was clean and pressed. Like I ain't never been in that house at all.

WHEN I GOT OUTSIDE, MRS. COBB WAS ALREADY behind the wheel of the motorcar. She had on a wide-brimmed hat with a netting that fell right in front of her eyes. In her lap was the shotgun.

Patrick opened the motorcar door and motioned for me to get in. "You remember what I told you, child. Get yourself back to Gee's Bend. Don't say nothing except yes'm and no'm."

"What's that, Patrick?" Mrs. Cobb called over the sound of the motor.

"Not a thing, Mrs. Cobb. Just helping the child get in."

I slid across the leather seat as Patrick closed the door behind me. The motorcar didn't have a top, so the seat was warm from the sunlight streaming onto it. I wasn't ready for the way the whole motorcar shuddered. It felt like I was in a nice warm nest that happened to be in a real shaky tree. My heart shuddered right along with it.

Then, with a jerk, we was moving. Mrs. Cobb pressed pedals with her feet and used her gloved hands to steer the wheel. Behind us the big house got smaller and smaller.

Look at me, I wanted to wave and shout. Across the river and riding in a motorcar. It was turning into some story, and I didn't have no idea how I was gonna fit it all into my quilt. But with Mrs. Cobb's fancy napkin to add to my bundle, I was sure gonna try.

The motorcar bumped along for what seemed like hours. Wasn't no talking due to the noise. I braced myself with my feet to keep from sliding into Mrs. Cobb's shotgun whenever we hit them rough spots in the dirt road. And rocks was the worst, on account of the way they lifted me right up and out of my seat. Then there was the bugs that kept getting in my eye.

I wished I had me a hat like Mrs. Cobb's. And I wished my teeth would stop rattling. Seemed like every bump and bounce set 'em off again. It was making my belly feel sick.

Was we ever gonna get to Camden? I reckon that ferry sure did take me a long way downriver. Or else them miles just seemed longer when you was bouncing around in a motorcar. I didn't say nothing about it to Mrs. Cobb, but I'd just as soon have walked all the way to Camden.

When I got tired of watching the fields go by, I rested my head against the seat and closed my eyes. I was about to drift off when Mrs. Cobb tapped my knee with her finger and pointed toward a group of houses on the right side of the street. They was big like Mrs. Cobb's house but lined up in a row like the cabins in Gee's Bend. I reckon you could fit four of our cabins into one of them houses. And seemed like every one of 'em was wrapped in a big wide porch that had fans hanging from the ceiling. I reckon them fans was mighty fine during summertime.

Mrs. Cobb turned left at the next street. There was a white painted sign that said WELCOME TO CAMDEN. And right there on the corner was the Wilcox Hotel. Next to the hotel was Dunn's Gulf Service Station, just like Daddy said. Across the street was Camden National Bank and W. E. Cook's. I could see in the window some of them fancy coats just like the one in the newspaper ad at home.

I didn't need nobody to tell me this was the main street in Camden. And sure enough, next thing I saw was a street sign painted Broad Street. Which meant this was where I would find Doc Nelson.

I couldn't believe how crowded the street was. I didn't like the way the motorcars and horses and wagons was going every which way. It was like my eye couldn't move fast enough to keep up with it all.

There was a few folks that looked like me, but most folks was shades of white. One man carrying a load of cotton in his wagon looked more red than anything else. His neck and arms looked like they had been just about burned up by the sun.

I rubbed my feet together. Whatever the color, they all had shoes. Not a single one of 'em was barefooted. And the clothes they was wearing covered their arms and legs and didn't look to be patched up or let out. Most of the men wore suits and hats, and the women's dresses were cut out of crisp cloth that kept its shape. Not like my old sack dress at all.

All the stores along Broad Street practically sparkled with their shiny windows and fresh-painted white trim. And the whole way was lined with streetlamps that had real electric bulbs. It was just like in the pictures Teacher showed us at school, only brighter. Wasn't none of the peacefulness of Gee's Bend. Seemed like everybody was moving, and I couldn't keep one noise separate from the next. No wonder Ruben didn't like it. Even I wanted to get out of there just as fast as I could.

Soon as Mrs. Cobb got the car parked and her hat off, I reached past the shotgun and patted her leg. "Thank you, Mrs. Cobb, for bringing me to Doc Nelson's office." I couldn't see the doctor's office, but I knew it had to be close. Wasn't but a few more buildings before Broad Street came to an end. "My daddy will thank you. And my mama, too, just as soon as she gets better."

Mrs. Cobb grabbed hold of my hand and squeezed. At first her glove felt soft against my fingers, and my heart flooded with gratefulness for all she'd done. Then the squeezing got harder. She was squeezing so tight I just about couldn't feel my fingers no more.

I tried to pull away, but Mrs. Cobb wasn't letting me go noplace.

"Mrs. Cobb?"

She wouldn't look at me. I reckon that's when I knew for sure something was wrong.

"Hush up, girl." The hard edge was back in her voice, and she had a mean look in her eye. *A rattlesnake ready to strike.* "We're not going to Doc Nelson's, Ludelphia Bennett. We're going to the store to look at the ledger. So I can decide what to do with you."

The ledger. Dear Lord. My face froze and I stopped trying to pull my hand away from Mrs. Cobb. Wasn't no doubt about it now. She was *the* Mrs. Cobb, wife of Mr. Cobb, the boss man who owned all the land we worked.

A picture of the armadillo with its insides spilling out came into my head. Didn't matter that she had given me a fancy napkin or a drink of Coke. Ruben had warned me. And Patrick had warned me.

Oh, Mama! Tears collected in the corners of my eyes. What was wrong with me that I didn't listen to the things folks told me?

I shook my head. I'd come all this way to save my mama from dying. Wasn't nobody gonna keep me from finding Doc Nelson. Not Mrs. Cobb or nobody. I yanked my hand hard as I could. When it didn't come loose, I yanked it again and again.

But wasn't no way out of Mrs. Cobb's grip. Her big piano hands held so tight to mine it felt like every little bitty bone was getting crushed.

Before I knew it, Mrs. Cobb was dragging me out of her side of the motorcar. My knees bumped up against the steering wheel, and I could hardly hold on to my quilt bundle. Beside us a rusty-colored horse was hitched to a post. It pushed its ears back and danced around in the dirt when I hit the street and Mrs. Cobb slammed the motorcar door behind me.

I might have screamed if not for the white lady and her little boy that was standing right in front of us. The boy pointed at me and said, "Look, Mama, it's a pirate!" I wanted to bury my head in my arms, but I couldn't, on account of Mrs. Cobb's hand. I wasn't no better off than a rabbit with its foot stuck in a trap, and now folks was poking fun at my eye patch.

I didn't hear what the lady said as they hurried off. Didn't matter nohow because I couldn't think of nothing but how stupid I was to get in that trap in the first place. And how in the world was I gonna get out of it?

Just ahead was a door that had CAMDEN MERCANTILE painted on the glass. Everything we ever had that we didn't make or grow ourselves came right from this store. All the seeds and tools for planting the fields. The pot for cooking soup. Mama's umbrella. This here was the place Daddy came to settle up his account with Mr. Cobb. Wasn't no good news coming out of this place lately, just Mr. Cobb telling Daddy how much we owed.

I wiped the tears from my cheeks as Mrs. Cobb held her shotgun in one hand and pulled me through the door with the other. Wasn't no telling what she would decide to do with me.

As Mrs. Cobb dragged me to the back of the store, my

eye got wide at the sight of all them bright bolts of cloth and shiny steel tools. I knew just what I'd do with all that cloth. I'd make new dresses for me and Mama and Rose, and wasn't no telling how many quilts I could make.

Overhead, more electric bulbs lit up row after row of canned goods that was labeled with colorful pictures. Down low was bins filled with rice and meal and flour. Even after that big breakfast Mrs. Cobb fed me, my belly still started churning just at the sight of all that food.

I couldn't believe how much stuff was packed in one room. Wasn't no need for a garden with a store like this one. I reckon there was enough food in Camden Mercantile to feed Mama and Daddy and Ruben and the Pettways too. We could live for years inside that store.

Back, back we went, past a rack of fancy dresses and denim britches and a shelf that had nothing but shoes on it. Men's work boots and shiny black shoes and little girl shoes too. I wanted to touch 'em, but Mrs. Cobb slapped my hand away.

"Get me the ledger," Mrs. Cobb said to a half-bald man that wasn't much taller than me. "Look for 'Bennett.' From Gee's Bend."

"Of course, Mrs. Cobb," the man answered.

I knew right away it wasn't Mr. Cobb. Because Ruben

said Mr. Cobb looked like a hog that's done ate too much. And wasn't nothing big about this man. He looked like a newborn rabbit that ain't never left its den.

If I could just talk to Mr. Cobb. Maybe I could get him to understand the only reason I came to Camden was to help save Mama from dying. That I didn't mean no harm sleeping in the barn. Maybe he could help get Mrs. Cobb's mind straight so she wouldn't look at me so mean.

I lifted my chin. Wasn't no time to be silent. Besides, what worse could Mrs. Cobb do to me than just about break all the bones in my hand? "I'd like to speak to Mr. Cobb," I said. "He's the boss man, and my daddy would want me to speak to the boss."

I held my breath as a look passed between Mrs. Cobb and the man flipping the pages of the book.

"You tell her, Mr. Miller," Mrs. Cobb said, finally letting go of my hand and shoving me forward. I wiggled my sore fingers to make sure they still worked.

I stared at Mr. Miller as he rubbed the top of his nose and squeezed his eyes tight. When he opened 'em, he looked at me hard. "Mr. Cobb is dead. Put him in the ground a week ago. Same day our new president was elected, Mr. Franklin Delano Roosevelt. I reckon you'd have a better chance of talking to Mr. Roosevelt than Mr. Cobb."

Mr. Cobb, dead? "How come we ain't heard it in

LEAVING GEE'S BEND

Gee's Bend?" Something that important, Daddy surely would have talked about it if he knew.

"It's not my job to tell folks," Mr. Miller said. "That's what newspapers are for."

I scratched under my eye patch. That wasn't how we got our news in Gee's Bend. Now, why wasn't Aunt Doshie gossiping about important things like Mr. Cobb dying instead of silly rumors about Etta Mae being a witch?

And poor Mrs. Cobb. No wonder she wasn't acting right. Why, Mama would be about half crazy herself if Daddy up and died.

"Mrs. Cobb," I said, turning toward her. What was it Mama always said at funerals? "I'm sorry for your loss. I ain't never met Mr. Cobb, but my daddy said he was a real good boss man. Real good." Mrs. Cobb didn't say a word. Just kept holding herself stiff.

I wanted to ask what it was that killed him. He wasn't coughing up blood, was he? They wasn't calling it pneumonia? I wanted to know everything so I could tell Daddy just as soon as I got back to Gee's Bend. But it wasn't the right time. I didn't need Mama there to tell me that. So I turned back to Mr. Miller.

"You the new boss man?" I asked him. "You the one Daddy will come to now for seed and fertilizer sacks?"

Mr. Miller shook his head and rubbed his chin. Like he was deciding what to say next. The whole time, Mrs. Cobb stayed real quiet.

"She got a name?" Mr. Miller said to Mrs. Cobb. Like I wasn't even there. Why didn't he just ask me?

"Ludelphia Bennett," I said in a rush. Wasn't no need for Mrs. Cobb to speak for me. And suddenly I wanted to tell Mr. Miller everything. If I could just make him understand I didn't mean no harm.

"My mama's real sick," I said. "And I came to Camden to fetch Doc Nelson. Only the ferry broke loose from the cable and I ended up way downstream." I looked over at Mrs. Cobb. She had both hands on the shotgun. I knew whatever I said next had to be just right.

"And Mrs. Cobb, she's been so kind to me. Took me up to the big house for breakfast and a Coke to drink. Then she carried me over here in her motorcar. Can't tell you how grateful I am."

Mrs. Cobb banged the gun against the floor, making me jump. "Don't you be fooled, Mr. Miller!" she said. "You see that eye patch?" She leaned toward him till there was only inches between their faces. "She's one of them. I just know it!"

"Now, Mrs. Cobb." His hands got fidgety and he

backed away. "The girl just wants to get a doctor for her mama. No harm in that, now, is there?"

Mrs. Cobb's face turned red, and it looked like she was about to explode. The blood rushed into my head, and I knew I had to get out of there. This could be my only chance.

Fast as I could, I turned on my heel and headed for the door.

Mrs. Cobb's voice roared above the slap of my feet on the floor. "Ludelphia Bennett, you get back here! I'm not finished with you yet!"

Wasn't no way I was stopping. Didn't matter what Mrs. Cobb said.

"Stop her, Mr. Miller! You got to stop her!" Mrs. Cobb said, her voice snapping like a quilt on a clothesline.

"Now, Mrs. Cobb. That girl hasn't done a thing to hurt you or nobody else. You just need to clear your head."

"That girl's from Gee's Bend!" Mrs. Cobb's voice came out in a screech. "You heard her say it. Just look at her, Mr. Miller, you just look!"

All my muscles ached and strained as I started to run. Wasn't no time to think. I had to get out of that store!

Just as I was reaching for the handle, the door swung open, pushing me back inside the store. Two ladies that was talking to each other came right inside. They wasn't paying a bit of attention. Of course I don't reckon they was expecting a little black girl to be making her escape at the exact time they was coming in the store to do their shopping.

If I could just get outside, I could find the doctor's office. I aimed for the space between the ladies and the door frame. Just when I thought I had it, the lady in the cream-colored dress shifted. I tried to stop myself, but it was too late. I slammed right into her, then she slammed into the other lady, and next thing I knew we was all falling.

Soon as I hit the floor, I could taste blood in my mouth where I had bitten my tongue. As I worked to get my feet under me, I realized my hands was empty. The fall had caused me to lose my quilt top. It had landed just a few feet away.

When I reached for it, my backside bumped the rack that was holding all the cloth. One after the other, them bolts came crashing down like bales of hay tumbling off a wagon. I was being buried alive!

After the last one fell, I cracked open my eye. Mrs. Cobb was standing with her arms crossed, looking on as Mr. Miller ran toward me.

Mama always said talking about fire don't boil the pot. If I was gonna get away, I needed to move now. So I pushed off the heavy bolts of denim, then I started to kick. Just like I was back in that river fighting for air. I reached and grabbed till one bolt of soft cotton shifted just enough for me to wiggle my hips. With one more big kick, the rest of them bolts slid right off me.

Just before Mr. Miller could get to me, I picked myself up off the floor and scooted past the two ladies, who was huddled together like they was scared for their lives. As I climbed over the mountain of stripes and calico and polka dots, I grinned because I was almost there. I was almost out of that store.

Wasn't till I got outside that I saw my hands was empty. My heart just about stopped beating right then and there. I didn't have my quilt top no more. But wasn't no going back for it. Had to find Doc Nelson. Had to find him now.

The Angel

OUT ON THE SIDEWALK, I TURNED FIRST TO THE right. There was a door that said ATTORNEY AT LAW. Beside that was a second door with a window and a wooden sign painted DOCTOR.

"Doc Nelson!" I said, pushing open the door. Above my head a little bell rang, but seemed like I was the only one that heard it. The room buzzed with the voices of ladies standing together in small groups. They was so busy visiting they didn't even notice me come in.

It was just like the cabin on Sunday afternoons when Mama would meet up with all the other ladies in Gee's Bend to put a quilt up in a frame. Once all the pieces was stitched together on the quilt top, then everybody worked together to beat the cotton down and stuff it between the top and bottom layers. There might be ten different needles working on the same quilt, and there was always a bunch of laughing and talking. Mama let me help some-times. But most times I just watched.

As I made my way into the doctor's office, I spotted on the far wall a poster that had a lady on it like I ain't never seen before. Her arms was spread wide, and she was dressed all in white with a little hat on her head that had a red cross on it. There was another sign just below it that said JOIN THE RED CROSS AND HELP THE DISTRESSED AND NEEDY. And below that was a small locked cabinet marked MEDICINE.

As my heartbeat slowed and the voices faded, it was like that lady was calling to me. Wasn't I distressed and needy? It was like she was an angel, and I couldn't help it, I was walking toward her. Didn't have no idea how a poster could help me. But there was something about it that made me all fluttery inside. And it made me think of Etta Mae. About all the times she took care of me.

Wasn't nothing of the devil in Etta Mae. I was sure of it. All that witch business was just crazy talk. This here was where Etta Mae belonged. On a poster like this one.

"Darlin'?" a lady said as she touched my arm. She had a freckled face with round cheeks. "You sure you're in the right place? This is a Red Cross drive."

Red Cross? Just like on the poster. "But the door said doctor. I'm here to see Doc Nelson."

"That right? Well, come on in. My name is Evelyn. I'm the doctor's wife." She took my hand and led me away from all them ladies through another door.

"Now," she said once the door was closed and there wasn't so much noise, "the doctor will be back in just a little while. He had to go check on the Patterson boy. Twelve years old and just put a nail right through the palm of his hand."

I sank down to the floor. I came all this way and Doc Nelson wasn't even here?

"Now, now," Mrs. Nelson said. "The doctor will be back in no time. Don't you worry about a thing." She patted the top of my head like I was a puppy, then stepped toward the counter that was in the corner of the room. "Can I offer you a piece of pound cake while you wait?" She held in her hands a tarnished silver tray. "Come on, now. It's fresh made."

I wiped my nose against my sleeve, then looked up at her. Mama always said it was rude to stare, but I ain't never seen so many freckles. They covered her nose and forehead and neck. And they was almost the exact same shade as her reddish-brown hair.

"Well, I'll just have myself a piece while you're deciding," Mrs. Nelson said as she picked up a piece of cake.

"Mmm," she said, closing her eyes. "I mean, that's good." She swallowed and wiped the crumbs from her bosom. "Now, why don't you tell me who you are." She looked at me expectantly as she folded her hands in her lap. Even her hands had freckles on 'em.

"Ludelphia Bennett," I said, putting my hands in my lap the same way she did hers. "From Gee's Bend. My mama's real sick, so I came to fetch the doctor."

"That right?" She picked up another piece of cake with her fingers and pushed it toward me. I wasn't a bit hungry, but I took it from her anyway and placed it on my tongue.

That cake fell to pieces in my mouth. I ain't never had a slice of pound cake so light and fluffy. I worked it around slowly in my mouth, tasting each flavor. First lemon, then vanilla, then a hint of cinnamon. Then I reached for the other piece.

Mrs. Nelson didn't say nothing else till I had eaten the last crumb. Just sat there watching.

"Thank you, ma'am," I said as I wiped the corner of my mouth. "That's some mighty fine pound cake."

Mrs. Nelson nodded. "Now, what's this about your mama?"

I patted the place where my pocket used to be. Then

I remembered. I'd stitched the pocket into my quilt top when I was drying out after my ride down the river. And now my quilt top was lying on the floor of Camden Mercantile.

I slapped the chair bottom. How was I gonna get it back? And how was I gonna tell Mrs. Nelson my story without stitching? It was like I needed the rhythm of that needle going in and out to calm myself enough to talk.

I thought of the blood coming out of Mama's mouth. Wasn't no choice, really. I just had to start talking. I just had to set my mind to it and tell Mrs. Nelson the whole story.

So that's what I did. I told Mrs. Nelson about the devil's lye and baby Rose being born and Etta Mae helping. I told her about the blood and about Aunt Doshie coming but not being able to help. I told her about the ferry and the river and barn and Patrick and Mrs. Cobb and the witches of Gee's Bend. It was like that pound cake let my tongue loose.

All the while, Mrs. Nelson's eyes never left me. When I finally finished, she took a deep breath and let it out real slow.

"Ludelphia, I'm sorry to have to tell you this." She shot her eyes down at her lap, then back at me. "But there's not a thing in this world Doc Nelson can do for your mama."

What do you mean? is what I wanted to say. Doc Nelson can't help Mama? But he's a doctor! He's the one Etta Mae told me to come get.

But wasn't no time for me to get the word out before there was a knocking at the door. Then a white-haired lady poked her head in.

"Evelyn, we need you in here. It's just about time for the drawing. And Mrs. Cobb is here. Said she wants to give a big donation!"

I jerked my head up. Mrs. Cobb? Dear Lord, after what I done to her store, she'd kill me for sure.

"Is that so?" Mrs. Nelson said, giving me a quick look and placing her hand on my shoulder. "Well, bless her heart. After all that's happened." She shook her head. "You tell her I'll be right out. And the Red Cross thanks her!"

Soon as the door was shut, Mrs. Nelson grabbed my shoulders and looked me in the eye. "Don't you worry, darlin'. I won't let anything bad happen to you. You just stay right here, and I'll go out and talk to Mrs. Cobb. Surely she won't hold a little mess in her store against you. That could've happened to anybody!"

"But, Mrs. Nelson, she's got a gun. And she thinks I'm a witch! I ain't never seen somebody so mad, not in my whole life!"

Mrs. Nelson crushed me against her and rested her chin on the top of my head. "Don't you worry, Ludelphia. You just wait here."

As the door shut behind her, everything quieted. All them voices died down, and Mrs. Nelson began to speak.

"Welcome, everyone, to the Red Cross drive. As many of you know, 1932 is our centennial year here in Camden. And with the depression going on, it's been a hard year for lots of folks. The Red Cross needs your donations now more than ever. With your cash donation here today, not only do you get to feel the pleasure of providing food and clothing and medicine to the distressed and needy, your name will be entered in a drawing for this lovely fur coat!"

A fur coat! You could win a fur coat in a drawing?

There was a chorus of oohs and aahs coming from the other room. If there was ever a drawing in Gee's Bend, it was for pie or a ripe watermelon. Not a coat.

Oh, Mama. If Doc Nelson can't help you, what am I gonna do? If only I had my needle so I'd have something to do with my hands.

I laced my fingers together, then unlaced 'em. What was it Etta Mae said the day they came to take away the church piano after Reverend Irvin sold it for new church seats? "Don't matter none," she said. "I'll just play it in my head."

And that's just what she did. There was times when we was together that Etta Mae would close her eyes and start to swaying. Didn't need nobody to tell me she was playing that piano.

Ain't nobody in the world can stop you from doing what you want to in your head. Ain't nobody can take hold of your thoughts, no matter what's happened. So while Mrs. Nelson talked and all them ladies listened, I closed my eyes and started stitching.

In my mind I picked up the quilt top from the floor of Camden Mercantile and held up the pieces I'd done stitched together. I turned it around and over till I had a clear picture of just how it looked so far.

My eye popped open. It wasn't right. Something about the quilt top just wasn't right. No matter which way I turned it, it just didn't look the way I wanted it to.

I leaned my head back against the wall and looked up at the ceiling. It was a flat white ceiling, just like at Mrs. Cobb's house. Not a trace of color on it. I squeezed my eyes shut and what came to me was the river. The brown water and orange dirt and blue sky. I held my breath till my chest ached same as it had when I was still underwater.

Mama always said it wasn't never too late to start over when you was piecing a quilt. When the colors was off and the seams didn't quite match up, wasn't nobody to stop you from taking it apart and starting over. The important thing was to do it right.

I couldn't think of but one thing to do. If it was true that Doc Nelson couldn't help my mama, then I had to get my quilting things back. I just had to. So I could pull them stitches out and start over again.

Dear Lord, I'm begging you! Please help me get Mama's quilt back. Help me get it right.

I knew now that the pieces from Mama's apron was meant to go in the middle. It all started with Mama and would work itself out from there.

In my mind, I stitched. Worked that needle in and out, in and out. I stitched and waited and tried to forget what Mrs. Nelson said about Doc Nelson not being able to help. Tried to rearrange the words till they meant what I wanted 'em to mean. Paid attention only to the picture in my head and stitched like I ain't never stitched before.

Blue Handkerchief

NEXT THING I KNEW, THERE CAME A KNOCKING on the door that sent all them stitches right out of my head. What if it was Mrs. Cobb? What if she wasn't coming to give a donation but was coming after *me*?

As the door opened, I scrambled to my feet. I'd outrun her once, and I'd do it again if I had to.

"Evelyn said you needed a doctor?" My mouth dropped open. It wasn't Mrs. Cobb. It was a man with thick brown hair that was shot all through with silver. And he was wearing a white coat. It had to be Doc Nelson!

My heart pounded as he strode through the doorway, his black shoes coming down firm and heavy. This here was the reason I had come such a long way. This man.

With Mrs. Nelson right behind him, the doctor squatted down and smiled just enough to show a dimple in his left cheek. "Is it your eye?" Wasn't no shock in his face at all as he studied my eye patch. Just matter-of-factness.

Tears gathered in my throat. "Nossir. It's worse than that." Then my nose started to run.

He pulled from his coat pocket a small blue handkerchief and pressed it into my palm. "Take this."

As tears slipped down my face, I curled my fingers around that thin scrap of cloth. It wasn't my quilt top, but it was something warm and solid. And smooth as a dogwood petal, like he'd been carrying it in that coat for years.

"Her name's Ludelphia," Mrs. Nelson said, her voice gentle. "Her mama's real sick, and she's come all the way from Gee's Bend to fetch you." Mrs. Nelson shook her head and lifted her eyebrows as she said it.

This was when he was gonna tell me no. But I couldn't let him. I wasn't gonna give him the chance.

I stood up and braced my legs the way Delilah does when she sees Daddy getting out the harness. Didn't matter what Mrs. Nelson said before. I was ready to fight if that's what it took.

"Doc Nelson," I said, ignoring the urge to scratch under my eye patch, "I need you to come back with me to Gee's Bend. Don't you tell me you can't."

The doctor chuckled. "Well, first you got to tell me

what the problem is. What exactly is wrong with your mama?"

"First it was just a cough. But soon as the baby came, everything got worse." I swallowed. "When I left, she couldn't hardly breathe and she was coughing up blood."

The doctor's mouth settled into a straight line. "And the baby?"

"Rose? Ain't a thing wrong with her. Was taking milk from a washcloth when I left."

"Good, good." Doc Nelson flashed his dimple, then his face got serious again. "If I was guessing, I'd say your mama's got pneumonia. You heard of pneumonia?" When I nodded, he went on. "It's real hard to treat. Doctors have been working on making some new medicine." His voice got real soft. "But it's not ready yet, Ludelphia. I'm sorry, but the best thing for her is rest. Rest and soup and anything you can do to make her breathing easier."

If he'd stabbed me it would have hurt less than hearing those awful words again. Those words that meant Aunt Doshie was right, Mrs. Nelson was right, and leaving Gee's Bend hadn't been nothing but a waste of time.

I wanted to scream, but my voice came out in a whimper. "Please, Doc Nelson. Just come to Gee's Bend. Just come and look in on Mama and say for sure."

Doc Nelson sighed then. It was one of them sighs I'd

heard from Daddy so many times. I knew now it was the sound of giving up. "I can't do that, Ludelphia. Much as I'd like to help your mama, I can't just leave. Not with three babies due any day and no other doctor for miles."

It was like my heart fell right out of my chest and Doc Nelson had just stomped on it with both feet.

"But what about Mama?" I looked from one to the other. "She might die if you don't come. That's the reason I came all this way to get you."

Doc Nelson reached for my hand, but I pulled away. "I promise to come just as soon as I can, Ludelphia. Just as soon as the ferry's up and running again and I can get another doctor to be here for my patients."

I was so mad I couldn't speak. It was like the tears had burned a hole in the back of my throat. Doc Nelson was just doing his job. But it didn't change the fact that I had come all this way for nothing. And no one seemed to understand about Mama. How serious it was and how it was up to me to make it right.

The room was silent except for my tears. I swiped them away as fast as I could. Crying never helped nothing neither.

"Mrs. Cobb!" Doc Nelson said when someone from the other room pushed open the door.

At the sound of her name my shoulders tightened and I shrank back toward the wall.

Doc Nelson stood between me and Mrs. Cobb. "Haven't seen you since the funeral," he said. "Everything okay?"

With Doc Nelson blocking my view, I couldn't see nothing of Mrs. Cobb except her skirt and her hands. They was gripping that shotgun so hard her fingers was turning red. Didn't Mrs. Cobb ever go noplace without that thing?

"I just came over to collect Ludelphia," Mrs. Cobb said. "Thought I'd take her home with me tonight."

Mrs. Nelson threw her arm over my shoulders like she was a hen and I was her chick. But it still didn't stop me from shaking.

Doc Nelson scratched his head, then spoke in a low voice. "You sure that's a good idea, Mrs. Cobb? Now, I know it's been a difficult time since Mr. Cobb passed. Don't make sense for you to have to look after the girl at a time like this."

Mrs. Nelson squeezed my shoulder. "Listen to the doctor, Mrs. Cobb. I'm sure Ludelphia's family is worried sick about her. She needs to get on back to Gee's Bend."

Mrs. Cobb's eyes got small and beady. "You just don't

know who you're dealing with, do you? I'm here to tell you Ludelphia Bennett is a—" Mrs. Cobb stopped herself before she finished the sentence. She tightened her grip on the barrel of the shotgun. "Hmmm," she said, looking from the doctor to his wife.

When she spoke again, her voice had turned to syrup. "Now, you know well as I do it's a good forty miles to Gee's Bend by road. Too late in the day for Ludelphia to get back before it turns dark."

She was right. My legs got all wobbly like they was gonna fall out from under me. Wasn't no way for me to get back home till tomorrow. Not with the ferry lost someplace downstream. Dear Lord, why did Gee's Bend have to be so hard to get to?

My head got light then and I had to grab hold of Mrs. Nelson's middle to keep myself up. Wasn't no way I was gonna go with Mrs. Cobb. I'd take off running before I'd get back in that motorcar with her.

Mrs. Nelson pulled me to her, and I felt myself sink into her side. "I think we'll just keep her here with us, Mrs. Cobb. No need for you to trouble yourself. Especially after everything that's happened today."

How could I be mad when she and the doctor was trying so hard to keep me safe? I stayed close as Mrs. Nelson reached out and placed her freckled hand on top of Mrs.

Cobb's plain one. "I am so sorry for your loss, Mrs. Cobb. Especially coming so soon after little Sarah's passing. If there's anything I can do, anything at all, you just let me know."

Mrs. Cobb's snatched her hand away from Mrs. Nelson and focused her attention on me.

"You listen to me, girl." Mrs. Cobb shook her finger not two inches from my nose. "Mr. Cobb said for me to 'take care of the folks in Gee's Bend.' For years I've been telling him to cut you loose, that Gee's Bend ain't worth all the trouble. Don't you see? That's what killed him. Looking after all you sharecroppers and the store too."

She stopped to catch her breath, then started again. "How many times did I beg him to let you go? But no, he said. He said we got to take care of you. Well, not anymore. I got no use for you folks in Gee's Bend. I'm done."

Mrs. Cobb rubbed her eye with her fist. "Because of you witches I don't have no one now. No one at all."

Doc Nelson interrupted her then. "Go on now, Mrs. Cobb." His voice was quiet but firm, like he was talking to a small child. "You don't even know what you're saying. So much has happened. You need to go on home now and get some rest." The doctor took her arm and guided her toward the door.

This time she turned to go with no trouble at all. Her shoulders slumped forward and her head hung low. Doc Nelson opened the door, and I held my breath as I watched one big boot step through the doorway, then the other. I was just letting my breath out when she swung back around and drilled her eyes right into mine.

"I've seen the ledgers," she said, her lips curling into a snarl. "I know Mr. Cobb loaned you folks way more than you've been able to pay back." She tapped the barrel of the shotgun on the floor. "Not enough cotton in the whole state of Alabama to make good on those debts."

She blew her breath through her nose, then her voice turned to poison. "I'm coming to collect." She shook her finger in the air. "I'm coming to Gee's Bend, and I'm taking everything you got. Everything that belongs to *me*. Then you'll know what it feels like to have nothing."

As Mrs. Cobb stalked out of the room, her skirt swirled around them boots. My mind swirled too, and it was like I wasn't even in the doctor's office no more.

Instead I was at home surrounded by the papered walls of the cabin. Wasn't really the walls that stood out, it was the blue flowers and bright orange trim on Mama's Housetop quilt. It was the same quilt I'd used to catch Rose when she was being born. And it was the same quilt

Mama liked to spread on the cabin floor after supper for telling stories.

As them colors streamed through my mind, I remembered the most terrible story of all, the one Mama said showed how the devil lives in some folks.

"Long before you or me was here," Mama always said, "and even before my mama and her mama was here, Big Mama lived in Africa."

Then she told the story about how Big Mama was captured while she was sleeping, and put in chains. How they marched for days all across Africa before they got to the coast. How the white men put them in pens like they was cows waiting for slaughter.

When Big Mama saw the ship come into the harbor with its red flags flying and its red ribbons tied to the railing, she screamed for her sisters that was left behind. She didn't know where that ship was going, but she knew it wasn't noplace she wanted to go. But wasn't no way she could have imagined America or how awful the trip would be.

For weeks Big Mama sat chained in the dark belly of the ship, her body crammed against other bodies that was naked and sick and starving. Mama always said it was them red flags that kept Big Mama from dying on that ship. She just blocked out everything else that was happening, the stench and the screaming and the sickness, and kept her mind on them flags flapping in the wind. She decided she was gonna breathe fresh air again and see an open sky and feel warm sunshine on her cheeks. Wasn't nobody gonna take that from her.

Sitting there on the floor of Doc Nelson's office with all them colors from Mama's quilt bouncing around in my head, I understood for the first time it wasn't the red flags that saved Big Mama's life. It wasn't something as plain as pieces of red cloth. It was something inside Big Mama, something strong and stubborn. It was about not giving up, no matter what.

I couldn't understand why Mrs. Cobb would want to hurt me or nobody else in Gee's Bend. But I reckon some things just can't be understood. And if Big Mama could live through all that happened on that ship, I could live through whatever happened next.

Doctor or no doctor, quilt or no quilt, wasn't no time for me to give up. No, now was the time for me to get myself home. So I could help Mama. So I could warn all of Gee's Bend about Mrs. Cobb coming to collect.

A Needle and a Spool of Thread

AS MRS. NELSON FINISHED UP WITH THE RED CROSS drive, Doc Nelson sat with me in the little room.

"Don't you worry about Mrs. Cobb," he said. "Once she sleeps on it she'll see what a bad idea it is to go Gee's Bend." Then he smiled just enough for the dimple to show.

I rubbed the back of my neck and moved my head from side to side. I wanted so much to believe what he said. But I just couldn't. Not after all I'd seen.

Doc Nelson checked the time on his watch. "Eleven o'clock already?" He ran his hand through his hair like he was worn out. "Ludelphia, I've got to go check in on Mrs. Cook. Amos came by and said little Annie's throat is so sore she's stopped eating." He looked at his watch again. "You'll be okay till Evelyn gets done?"

I nodded and Doc Nelson scooted out the door. Once

he was gone, I walked around the hard wood table that was in the center of the room. There was a little pillow on one side, I reckon for putting your head. Was that the table I'd have lain on if Mama and Daddy had brought me to Doc Nelson after the eye accident? Is that the table where Mama would lay if she was here?

I propped my elbows on the table and let my face rest in my hands. Oh, Mama. I'm sorry I've gone and made such a mess of things. You just got to hang on till I get back. Then everything will be different. I won't sass you no more. I'll do just what you tell me, even if it means wearing this stupid old eye patch for the rest of my life. I just want to be home with our whole family in one room.

I jumped when the door cracked open. "Thank you for coming!" Mrs. Nelson's voice called. "See you next week! Good-bye!" She flashed me a smile. "How 'bout that? Got more donations than ever! Over three thousand chapters of the Red Cross all across the country, but every year ours is one of the most generous."

"That mean you'll be able to help lots of folks?"

"That's right. Never know when a drought will settle in or when a tornado will come ripping through. Soon as the Red Cross hears about it, they send food and clothing and tools for rebuilding or replanting or whatever else it is that's needed." Mrs. Nelson sighed and put her arm

LEAVING GEE'S BEND

around my shoulders. "You should see some of the letters folks write! It would break your heart for sure."

I bit my lip. "Folks write letters telling about their troubles and the Red Cross sends help?"

"That's right. Whenever something comes along that folks can't handle themselves."

"I ain't never heard of such a thing, Mrs. Nelson."

Mrs. Nelson squeezed my shoulder. "Everybody needs help from time to time."

Wasn't no doubt about that. And right now was one of those times.

I leaned my head against her arm. "Mrs. Nelson, it's time for me to go home. I've got to get back to Mama and baby Rose. I've got to warn 'em about Mrs. Cobb."

Mrs. Nelson pulled me closer to her. "I can't let you go, darlin'. You walking alone and night coming on? It wouldn't be safe. And I can't think of a soul who'd be willing to take you this late in the day. No, it would be best for you to wait till tomorrow." She patted my cheek. "But don't you worry, we'll figure something out. We'll get you home just as soon as we can."

I wiggled away from her. "But, Mrs. Nelson! I got to get back there. I got to get back to my mama."

"Darlin', I know you're missing your mama." Mrs. Nelson ran her hand along my arm. Then she looked at me hard, the way Mama did when I forgot to put on my eye patch. I reached up to make sure it was still there. "But you got to think it through. What would your mama and daddy say if I just turned you loose right now?"

I slumped again into the chair and balled the blue handkerchief in my hand. Mrs. Nelson was right. Wasn't nothing for me to do but wait till morning came. And me without my quilting things to help pass the time.

"Come on, now," Mrs. Nelson said. "You can help me."

I followed her through the door to the waiting room. Was it really the same room I came through earlier? Now that it was empty, it looked completely different. I hadn't even noticed how there was chairs lined up all along the walls when the room was full of them ladies.

I liked the way the Red Cross poster seemed to stand guard over the place. Like that angel was watching everything that happened.

By the time Doc Nelson got back, it was late afternoon and the waiting room was filled with all sorts of folks needing help. Mrs. Nelson said that's the way it happened most times. Nothing to do for hours, then they'd all come in at once.

The blacksmith came in with a gash in his leg that

LEAVING GEE'S BEND

needed stitching. He had white skin except for his hands. His fingers was almost all black, I reckon from working with fire so much. "Did a horse get you in the eye?" he said to me while Mrs. Nelson was fetching him a clean towel to press against the cut.

I took the chair beside him. "Nossir. Ain't got no horses. Just a mule named Delilah."

The blacksmith nodded. "I'd take a good mule over a bad horse any day."

Next, a white lady came in with a little boy in her arms that was whimpering and holding his ears. They sat in the far corner, clear across the room from me.

The poor mama looked about as bad off as he did, the way them dark circles was shadowing her eyes. I started to make silly faces like Etta Mae always done to distract me when I was sick, but Mrs. Nelson called me to her. "Probably best if you stay close to me, Ludelphia. Some folks won't know what to make of you."

So I followed Mrs. Nelson as she moved from patient to patient, chatting about how cold the winter might be and asking after the patients' husbands and wives and children. Wasn't nobody in that room she didn't know.

It was just like being at Pleasant Grove Baptist Church on a Sunday morning after the singing and sermon was done. Except I was the only one that was colored in the whole place. All the other folks that came into the doctor's office was white.

"Mrs. Nelson," I said, "is the white folks the only ones that get sick in Camden?"

Mrs. Nelson took my hand in her freckled one. "There's a separate waiting room in the back for colored folks. But not many of 'em come here. There's a colored doctor over in Selma that comes to town from time to time. Doc Nelson says that's who they go to most times when they get sick."

I didn't know what to think about that. Mostly it just made me miss Daddy and Ruben. And Mama, of course. I just wanted to go home, where things made more sense.

How long before Daddy would come after me? Wasn't likely that he'd be willing to move from Mama's side. Least not while she was still alive.

I stroked the blue handkerchief with my thumb. Daddy might not be able to come after me, but I bet he'd send somebody. Could be there was somebody on the way to fetch me right this very minute.

Unless—unless Mama didn't make it. I folded the worn blue cloth, then folded it again till it was as small as I could make it.

What would happen to Rose if Mama didn't get

better? Who would teach her all the things she needed to know? I tried to get a picture of Rose in my mind, but it wouldn't come. There was the shape of a baby, but the face was blurred.

I shook my head hard. I just had to get through the rest of the day and night. Then I could get back to Gee's Bend where I belonged.

Patients came and went until there was just two left. Doc Nelson was working so hard I ain't even seen him since he got back. Mrs. Nelson shuffled some paper around on the top of the desk, then sat down with a sigh. "How are you holding up?"

I lifted the blue handkerchief to my nose. "Be better if I hadn't dropped my quilting things when I was running out of Camden Mercantile."

Mrs. Nelson's eyes widened. "What, like a needle and a spool of thread?"

"Not a whole spool. But I did have some good pieces of cloth."

"Well, darlin', I wish you'd said something sooner. I would have been happy to go over there and get it for you."

Mrs. Nelson would have gotten it back for me? And I'd been sitting all this time with nothing to do when I could have been working on Mama's quilt.

Mrs. Nelson looked toward the window where the sky was turning purple and pink as the sun dropped down. "Reckon it's too late now. I saw Mr. Miller locking up the door about an hour ago."

I clamped my mouth shut. Everything that was important to me I'd somehow managed to mess up. Is that what it meant to be a witch? Things just always going the wrong way?

"So you like to quilt, do you?" Mrs. Nelson didn't even wait for me to answer, just opened a drawer and fumbled around with her fingers. Then she pulled out a spool of white thread and put it in my hand. "Hardly used. Bought it from Mr. Cobb one day when the doctor popped a button." She closed the drawer while I sat there watching.

"You know, Ludelphia, it's a real shame about Mr. Cobb." Mrs. Nelson leaned back in her chair. "Heart attack. Wasn't nothing to be done."

I unraveled a bit of thread, then rolled it back in. So it was a heart attack that killed Mr. Cobb.

"And I can't help but feel sorry for Mrs. Cobb," Mrs. Nelson said, giving me a quick look. "Must be hard for her to lose her husband so soon after that little niece of hers passed away. It's no excuse for the way she's acting, but I bet Mrs. Cobb's hurting real bad right now."

Well, she ain't the only one, is what I wanted to say.

"Grief can do crazy things to a person." Mrs. Nelson smoothed her skirt. "Mrs. Cobb, she's not in her right mind. She hasn't been right since even before little Sarah died." She clicked her tongue and tucked a strand of hair behind her ear. "Must be awful hard to want children and not be able to have them. And then to lose the one that comes closest to being your own."

As my hand closed around the spool of thread, I didn't know whether to say "thank you" or "please stop talking about Mrs. Cobb." I didn't know why Mrs. Nelson was telling me these things. Not when Mrs. Cobb was planning to take things from folks that ain't done a single bad thing to her.

But wait. Mrs. Cobb didn't have children? Then who was the baby in the picture on Mrs. Cobb's wall?

"Mrs. Nelson?" I rolled the spool of thread around in the palm of my hand, then pulled off the needle. Dear Lord did that needle feel good in my fingers. "What happened to her niece? Little Sarah?"

The corners of Mrs. Nelson's mouth turned down. "She died, darlin'. About a month ago down in Mobile while Mrs. Cobb was visiting. Just died in her sleep one night."

Mrs. Nelson sighed. "Doc Nelson said it just happens with babies sometimes. It's nobody's fault. But there was some talk that it was the doings of a witch." Mrs. Nelson looked me square in the eye. "Mrs. Cobb said it was a witch from Gee's Bend."

I gasped as the needle went right into my thumb. Etta Mae! Mrs. Nelson was talking about Etta Mae. I pressed my thumb with my other fingers to stop the bleeding. I couldn't even remember the last time I'd stuck myself.

The baby in the picture had to be Sarah. It had to be. And Etta Mae was the one hired to help care for her.

Mrs. Nelson put her hand on my knee. "Life sure is complicated, isn't it?"

Complicated wasn't a big enough word.

As I sucked on my sore thumb, I gripped the spool of thread. It wasn't right. So many folks dying. Mr. Cobb and little Sarah. Mama coughing up blood and baby Rose coming early and Etta Mae back so soon from Mobile. And me trying so hard to fix things but not fixing 'em.

Mrs. Cobb may have lost things, but that didn't give her no right to treat nobody the way she was treating me.

I looked close at my pricked thumb. There was a tiny hole in my skin, but it wasn't bleeding no more. If only everything else was that easy to fix.

I started again with the needle. Mama always said you

LEAVING GEE'S BEND

should live a life the same way you piece a quilt. That you was the one in charge of where you put the pieces. You was the one to decide how your story turns out.

Well, seemed to me some of them pieces had a mind of their own.

"WHAT'S FOR SUPPER?" DOC NELSON SAID AS HE closed the door behind the last patient.

Supper? Soon as the word entered my mind, my belly started to talk. I hadn't put a thing in my mouth since Mrs. Nelson's pound cake earlier that morning.

"Leftovers will have to do," Mrs. Nelson said, heading down the hallway. She paused someplace in the middle and looked back at me. "You coming, Ludelphia?" I real quick folded the needle and thread into the blue handkerchief and followed them through the last door on the right. The walls was plain white and pushed against the wall was a pine-plank table that reminded me of home.

Mrs. Nelson pulled a jug of milk from under the cabinet and poured it into three glasses. From the same cabinet she grabbed a pie tin and set it right in the center of the table. There was a cut of ham and some black-eyed peas.

"Save some room for dessert, now," she said and settled into a chair. "Doctor, say the blessing?"

I bowed my head. If Mama could have seen me, she would have been proud of how I closed my eyes and folded my fingers.

"Plenteous grace with thee is found, grace to cover all my sin. Let the healing streams around make and keep thee pure within. Amen."

"Amen," Mrs. Nelson added.

It wasn't nothing like the special blessing we said at home, where we named folks and said the exact things we was thankful for. But the food sure was plentiful. Even at Sunday dinner we didn't have a spread like this one. I reckon that's why it was so much quieter at the doctor's table. Less folks talking and more food to eat.

Things wasn't all fancy here the way they was at Mrs. Cobb's house. But I was still careful to keep my napkin in my lap and my mouth closed while I was chewing. Mama always said manners was appreciated no matter who you was with. So far it seemed to be true. Whether I was at Mrs. Cobb's table with the napkins folded into birds or talking to nervous Mr. Miller at Camden Mercantile or here with the Nelsons, who couldn't look more different than me but treated me like I was just the same.

I reckon when you grow up in one place you just

naturally think every other place is the same as your home. I reckon it takes leaving to appreciate all the things about that place that make it special.

Dear Lord, did I want to go home.

As the Nelsons talked about the busy day, I ate till my plate was clean. Homesick or not, wasn't no way I could let any of that good food go to waste.

Soon Mrs. Nelson began to clear away the dishes. "Ludelphia, did you save room for a piece of my fresh-made apple pie?"

I licked my lips. "Yes'm, I always got room for pie."

The Nelsons both laughed. Seemed to me they liked to watch me eat.

Once the pie was gone, Doc Nelson leaned back in his chair and yawned. "We'll all sleep good tonight, won't we, Ludelphia?"

I nodded but I wasn't sure it was true. I had too many worries for sleeping good.

While Mrs. Nelson wiped down the table, Doc Nelson set up a cot for me right there in that same room. Then Mrs. Nelson covered it with crisp white sheets and a plain brown blanket. Wasn't nothing like one of Mama's quilts.

"You need us, we're in the next room," Mrs. Nelson said just before she turned out the light.

Then it was dark and I was alone again in a place that

wasn't my home. In a room that was filled with nothing but silence.

Then came a wailing sound from far-off outside. It wasn't an animal, and I didn't have no idea what it could be.

I sat straight up in my bed. "Mrs. Nelson!"

"What is it, darlin'?"

"That crying sound. What is it?"

She listened for a minute as the wailing stopped and started again. "That?" she said. "Why, that's a train, Ludelphia. There's a station over at Pine Hill." She bustled over and pulled the covers up to my shoulders. "You never heard a train blow its whistle before?"

I shook my head. So that's what a train sounded like! Wasn't nothing like I expected. It was such a lonely sound, when all this time I thought it would sound like the start of a grand adventure.

After Mrs. Nelson left me for the second time, I lay there in the dark with my eye wide open. Next door the doctor and Mrs. Nelson bumped around a bit, and I could hear the gentle rumble of their voices as they talked. But soon it was quiet. Wasn't no chickens clucking or water dripping. No snoring or coughing or rustling of arms and legs on the cornshuck mattress. It was quiet like I ain't never heard.

Soon my arms and legs felt heavy, even the air felt heavy coming in and out of my chest. The quiet was begging me to sleep, but I couldn't stop my mind.

It'd been three days since Rose was born. Was it only yesterday morning that I'd left Gee's Bend? If only there was some way for me to know what kind of shape Mama was in.

No matter what the doctor and Mrs. Nelson said, I was heading back to Gee's Bend the next morning. Wasn't nobody gonna stop me. I'd walk, I'd run, I'd hop on one foot if I had to. I was going home to our cabin with its colorful walls and the quilts stacked in the corners. Back to the sounds and smells and folks I loved best. Back to Delilah and chickens and the woodpile and fried salt pork for breakfast.

Maybe I couldn't save Mama. But I could still go home and hold baby Rose and smooth Mama's hair away from her face.

Please, Lord, let Mama still be alive when I get there.

As my eyelids finally closed, I saw not Mama, but Mrs. Cobb. Her skin was paler than ever, and her shotgun wasn't by her side no more. It was aimed straight at me.

The Letter

Next thing I knew Mrs. Nelson was shaking me awake. I could tell it was morning by the way sunlight was just barely coming into the room. I reckon without the sounds of the chickens and Mama banging around wasn't nothing to wake me up.

"Ludelphia Bennett, you listen to me." She looked toward the waiting room, then back at me. "I want you to take these two bottles of medicine."

Two bottles. Medicine.

I sat straight up in bed and rubbed the sleep from my eyes. "Yes'm?" In her palm was two brown glass bottles, each of them about the size of an inkwell.

She placed the bottles in my hands. "It's called morphine. Won't heal your mama, but it might ease her suffering just a bit."

As I wrapped my fingers around the cool glass, my

mind filled up with so many words I thought I might come to pieces. But I couldn't make a one of 'em come out of my mouth.

Mrs. Nelson didn't seem to notice. She was too busy fiddling with my eye patch that had slipped out from under the pillow. "Doc Nelson wouldn't want me giving you those bottles. Folks can get crazy once they've had morphine, then you take it away."

She slid the eye patch over my head, then pulled back the blanket. I didn't know what else to do, so I just focused on her freckles. "Darlin', I'm trusting you. Don't give your mama too much. Just a little teaspoonful at a time. And maybe, just maybe, it'll help give her body enough strength to pull through. Might take her months to get all the way better. But if she can just get past the worst of it, she'll be all right, Ludelphia. There's a chance she'll be all right."

"Yes'm," I said, my heart just about to burst. Mrs. Nelson wanted to help me so much she was doing something some folks might say wasn't quite right. Wasn't for me to say. All I knew was that if Mrs. Nelson said Mama had a chance of getting better, then Mama had a chance.

"Now, get on with you," she said as she handed me the blue handkerchief. "And take this lunch sack with you.

It's just a bit of ham and a biscuit, but it ought to hold you till you get home to your mama."

I threw my arms around her then. Wasn't no reason in the world for her to be so nice to me. Wasn't no law that said she had to help me at all. But here she was, helping me. "Thank you," I said.

She gave me a quick squeeze, then the metal frame of the cot squeaked as she stood. "Go on now, darlin', while the doctor's tending to Mrs. Johnson." Her eyes had tears in 'em and her voice cracked a little. "Just take a left at the end of Broad Street. Then that road will take you on up to Alberta. I reckon you know the way from there."

As I swung my legs around and set my feet on the floor, I wasn't worried about finding Gee's Bend. If I could get all the way here to Doc Nelson's, then I could sure find my way home. Especially when all my body parts suddenly felt electric, like a switch had been flipped and now my arms and legs was all lit up.

Maybe it wasn't a cure. But it was something. All I had to do now was hold tight to them bottles and fast as lightning carry them home.

I could hear my heart in my ears as I scooted down the hall to the waiting room.

Didn't matter that I hardly had no sleep, my legs felt

strong, like they could carry me anyplace. And when I saw that poster again with the lady that looked like an angel, a warm feeling spread all through my body.

I felt like I was lit up like one of them electric bulbs. And right then I knew there was something else I needed to do. I set the bottles on Mrs. Nelson's desk and picked up a notepad and a fresh-sharpened pencil. My hand started shaking soon as I started to write.

Dear Red Cross:

We need your help in Gee's Bend, Alabama. If you ain't heard of it yet, ask Mrs. Nelson. She'll tell you where it is. The reason I'm writing is because Mrs. Cobb said she's gonna take everything we got. And my Mama is real sick. I don't know if there is anything you can do to help her, but I just thought you should know. Please help us!

Signed,
Ludelphia Bennett

I folded the note and wrote on the outside "To: American Red Cross, From: Ludelphia Bennett." Wasn't nothing left for me to do now except give the letter to Mrs. Nelson.

"Mrs. Nelson," I called as I stuck my head out of the

doorway and looked down the hallway.

No answer. The doctor's office was completely quiet. Didn't need nobody to tell me she was gone. I reckon she didn't want to see me go.

All I had to do now was put it someplace Mrs. Nelson was sure to find it. Then when she turned over all the donations she'd collected from the Red Cross drive, she could give 'em my letter. And they would send help.

I glanced around the room. Where should I put it? Then I remembered the pound cake Mrs. Nelson gave me when I first came into the doctor's office.

The cake plate. Much as she loved her cake, Mrs. Nelson was sure to find it. But I wanted to be sure. So I folded the note one more time and wrote "To: Mrs. Nelson, From: Ludelphia." That way there wouldn't be no mistaking what it was.

Then I grabbed them bottles of medicine and slipped them inside the lunch sack with the blue handkerchief and spool of thread. I held that bag to my chest, and the little bell rang as I shot out of that door with its glass window and painted-on sign. I was going home to Gee's Bend!

The Long Road Home

IT WAS EARLY YET, SO WASN'T NO STORES OPEN ON Broad Street. But there was three big wagons parked right in front of Camden Mercantile. Then half a dozen men rode up on horseback. Some of 'em was white, some of 'em black.

Was they gonna go hunting? What else could be going on this early in the morning? Then I saw her, Mrs. Cobb. Oh, dear Lord. Couldn't mean but one thing.

As she walked from the store to the middle of the street, I could tell what she was fixing to do just by the way she was setting each boot so firm in the dirt. Then when she lifted her gun into the air, wasn't no doubt in my mind.

I covered my head with my arms to block the sound of the shot. Didn't help all that much. It still set my ears to ringing. I reckon it was loud enough to just about wake the whole town.

"See you in Gee's Bend!" she said, waving the shotgun in the air.

No, I wanted to shout. Not Gee's Bend. Now how was I gonna get there before Mrs. Cobb did? How was I gonna warn everybody?

As another horseman with a shotgun slung over his shoulder rode up, I ducked into the shadows. Didn't want Mrs. Cobb or nobody else to see me. "Where are the others?" the horseman called out.

"Rounding up a few more that need the work!" Mrs. Cobb said as Patrick came out of the store. "Patrick will take one wagon straightaway, and I'll be right behind in the other. Then we'll meet up at Pleasant Grove Baptist Church and set out from there."

The horseman tipped his hat. "That where we get paid? At the church?"

"No one gets paid until the job is done."

Dear Lord. They was going to the church? Wasn't no way for me to get to there before they did. Even with a head start them wagons would catch up to me in no time.

I hung my head and held tight to my bag. What was I

gonna do now? I had to get there somehow. Because Mrs. Cobb wouldn't be coming to Gee's Bend if not for me.

When I lifted my head, the air was full of dust and Mrs. Cobb was gone. The only one left in the street was Patrick sitting tall in the wagon, and he was waving something colorful in the air. As the dust settled, I could see it was about the size of a flag, and it looked like he was waving it at me.

I stepped away from the building and into the street. Soon as I did, Patrick started waving that flag even faster. Wasn't no doubt in my mind now that it was my attention he wanted.

"Yah," Patrick said to the horses, and they began to move toward me. As they got closer, I could see the flag had blue denim and white burlap and calico.

It wasn't a flag at all.

I wanted to jump and shout hallelujah! It was like a miracle, that quilt. I never expected to see it again. But there it was blazing in the morning light.

"It ain't right what she's doing," Patrick said once he got close to me. "It ain't right at all." Patrick took a quick look back toward Camden Mercantile and pulled back on the reins. "Be quick, now. Hop up and hide yourself in this wagon." He glanced toward the store and back again. "Got to keep yourself real flat. And not a peep out of you! You hear? If Mrs. Cobb finds out she'll get rid of me for sure."

I knew how much Patrick needed his job. Seven children. And here he was taking a chance on me?

Wasn't a thing I could think of to say how grateful I was. Wasn't no words for how I was feeling. So I just nodded. Then I gripped the lunch sack in one hand and pulled myself up with the other.

I got myself settled under a pile of rope quick as I could. Curled myself up into a ball with my face toward the back of the wagon so I could see the road.

"Yah," Patrick said, and the horses started walking. As they moved into a trot, I felt something soft flutter down onto my head.

All the pieces was there: the scraps of denim, the pocket from my dress, the strips I tore from Mama's apron. Even the needle was there, tucked in at the seam just the way I'd left it. I could smell Mama and river water and Mrs. Cobb's barn and my own sweat. I pressed it to my nose and sobbed.

For miles wasn't nothing to see from the back of that wagon except blue sky and empty cotton fields. Mrs. Cobb and the others was far enough behind us that it seemed like we was the only ones on the road. But I didn't dare poke my head up.

"You all right back there?" Patrick hollered over the noise of the wagon.

"Yessir," I hollered back.

"Just passed the sign for Alberta. 'Bout halfway there now."

Halfway? We was already halfway there? That meant we would soon be to Rehoboth. And after Rehoboth the road ended at Gee's Bend.

Them horses sure was fast. Not as fast as Mrs. Cobb's motorcar, but not slow like Delilah neither. Dear Lord, would I be glad to see Delilah.

I looked out the back of the wagon. I wish I'd seen the sign for Alberta. Was it white like the sign for Camden? Now I might never know. Once I got back to Gee's Bend, I didn't have no plans to ever leave again.

I bunched the quilt top and put it under my head. It helped soften the bumps, but I still felt like I'd been run over with the plow. Wasn't a part of my body that didn't ache from being bounced around in that wagon. But each roll of the wagon wheel, each bump and jolt, was bringing me closer to home. I could tell by the way the pine trees along the road was greener than they was before, the sky more blue. I sucked in the fresh-smelling air, and I knew we was getting close.

I kept a tight grip on the lunch sack. I pressed it

against my chest so I could feel each of them medicine bottles. They was there, safe and firm.

Please, Lord. Let me get there in time.

As the cotton fields turned to cornfields, I saw a flash of yellow in the ditch. Yellow like the yellow on Etta Mae's dress.

I real quick jerked my head up. "Etta Mae!" I said as the wagon kept moving away from her. Could it be?

As I pushed the rope off and got to my knees, the flash of yellow moved into the road. Something else moved with it.

I squinted my eye and looked hard as I could through the dust the horses and wagon was kicking up.

Not something, somebody.

"Stop the wagon, Patrick! We got to go back!"

"Ho!" Patrick called to the horses. "What's that, Ludelphia?"

"Look!" I pointed to where Etta Mae and Ruben was running toward us.

I couldn't keep from grinning. They had come after me. Etta Mae the witch and Ruben, who thought Gee's Bend was the best place ever. They was worried and had come to fetch me.

"Hurry!" I called to 'em. "Mrs. Cobb is on her way. We got to hurry."

As Ruben and Etta Mae scrambled into the back of the wagon, I told 'em about Mrs. Cobb. "She said we got to pay. That everybody in Gee's Bend got to make good on our debts."

Ruben looked at me hard. "Pay our debts with what?"

I didn't have no answer. But I sure had questions. "Ruben, you got to tell me about Mama. Is she still coughing blood?"

I held my breath for his answer, but it didn't come before Patrick started hollering. "Get low!" he said. Then he slapped the reins and the horses moved into a gallop.

"What's he going on about?" Etta Mae said, her face just inches from mine.

"He's talking about me. No telling what Mrs. Cobb might do if she knew he was carrying me in this wagon."

A light came into Etta Mae's dark eyes. "She think you a witch too?"

I nodded.

"Mercy, Ludelphia, I'm sorry to hear it! If baby Sarah hadn't died . . . I swear I didn't do nothing to make it happen. She just stopped breathing. Wasn't nothing I could do."

"Ain't nothing wrong with neither one of you," Ruben said. "Look, now. We got bigger things to worry about. You see?"

On the road behind us was a small cloud of dust that was getting bigger every second. Mrs. Cobb and the others was right behind us now.

Wasn't no talking the rest of the way to Gee's Bend. I still didn't have no idea how Mama was doing. And there was so much I wanted to tell 'em. Like about the medicine bottles and the quilt I was making for Mama. And the Coke and the armadillo and the motorcar.

I had more questions too. Like, what made 'em both come after me? Was Daddy mad about me leaving? What did he say when Ruben told him I'd run off? But mostly I just wanted to know about Mama. I needed to know she was okay.

Then my mind jumped to the very worst thing. What if the reason they came after me was because Mama didn't make it? What if this very minute, Mama was dead?

"Ruben," I said.

His eyes got small and he put his finger to his lips. When I peeked through the back of the wagon I could see why. There was three horsemen just a few feet behind our wagon.

In less than a minute, they was past us. Wasn't much longer after that when the wagon began to slow. I could tell by the trees along the road that we was coming up on the church.

Dear Lord, don't let 'em see us. Help us get ourselves out of this wagon with no more trouble from Mrs. Cobb.

"Ho!" Patrick shouted as he pulled the horses up next to the front steps of Pleasant Grove Baptist Church. My heart raced at the sight of them steps. The part that I could see through the slats in the wagon looked just like I remembered 'em.

I wanted to leap right out of that wagon. I wanted my feet on that ground. But Ruben's hand on my arm stopped me. We had to wait for just the right time so we could get out without nobody knowing.

I curled my fingers around the lunch sack. Wasn't no words for how bad I wanted to get out of that wagon. But we was surrounded on all sides by horsemen and wagons. Wasn't the right time. Not yet.

"Mrs. Cobb," Ruben mouthed, then jerked his head to the right. She was passing right beside us! I held my breath till I couldn't see her wagon no more. After a few seconds, she started shouting out instructions, and judging by the sound of her voice, she was a ways in front of our wagon. I imagined her with her ledger in one hand and shotgun in the other, and I knew now was the time. The sooner the better.

I wiggled my hips out from under the pile of rope and

LEAVING GEE'S BEND

eased myself out of the wagon. As Mrs. Cobb kept on with her instructions, Etta Mae and Ruben began to follow.

After all that bumping around in the wagon it was like my mind was all scrambled up and I didn't trust my legs. I balled the quilt top in my fist and dropped down to my hands and knees. It wasn't easy to crawl with the quilt top in one hand and that little sack in the other, but I did it. Then I hid myself in a patch of holly bushes that grew right alongside the road. When I looked back, Etta Mae and Ruben was right behind me. Wasn't long before the three of us disappeared into the woods.

As soon as we was far enough from the wagons, Ruben pulled us up short. "Here's what we got to do. Split up. That way we can warn more folks about what's about to happen."

"How much time do we have?" Etta Mae said.

"Looks like Mrs. Cobb's planning to go cabin to cabin," Ruben said, looking at me. "Which means it might take a little while for her to get all the way to ours."

"But what if they split up too?" I said. "There's so many of 'em, and if they split up the same way we do, then it won't take 'em long at all."

Ruben held out a hand to each of us, and me and Etta Mae both grabbed hold. "All right then," Ruben said.

"Etta Mae, you head toward the swamp, I'll go toward the fields. And, Lu, you start with Aunt Doshie and head toward home. Then the three of us, we'll meet up there."

It made my insides warm the way Ruben took charge like that. It made me feel safe, like nothing else bad could happen. "See you at home," I said, squeezing his hand. Then we was off, each of us running in different directions.

I stopped when I got to Aunt Doshie's front porch steps. "Aunt Doshie, Mrs. Cobb's come to collect on all the debts!"

"Mrs. Cobb?" she said, coming to the door with her long braid swaying and her mouth hanging open. "Here in Gee's Bend?"

"Best hide what you can." I made sure to look her in the eye so she'd have less to gossip about later. "She's got wagons and men. Said she's gonna take everything we got."

I took off running, my feet falling sure and steady on that orange dirt footpath I'd been running on my whole life. I held tight to my quilting things and kept the lunch sack pressed against my chest.

Each cabin I came to, I shouted out a warning as I passed. But I didn't stop running. I had to get home. I had to see Mama. I had to know she was alive.

Falling

NEWS SPREAD DOWN THE ROW OF CABINS FASTER than I could run. I reckon they heard me shouting, then took to telling one another themselves.

As I passed through the Pettways' yard into mine, one of the hogs squealed and rushed toward me. I gripped the lunch sack tight and lifted my arms to scare it back.

"Stupid hog," Mr. Pettway said, chasing it with a pitchfork. "It don't know it's better off in them woods."

I hadn't thought about hiding the animals. But I reckon Mrs. Cobb could say they was hers too. Now she'd have to catch 'em if she wanted to carry 'em away.

While Mr. Pettway herded the hogs, Mrs. Pettway dragged the ax in one hand and a hoe in the other. Looked like she was taking 'em to the outhouse.

"Where's Etta Mae?" she said.

I started running again. "She's on her way."

I wanted to tell Mrs. Pettway wasn't nothing to them rumors about Etta Mae being a witch. I wanted to tell her it was just bad luck. Wasn't no reason to worry. But I didn't have time to talk.

"Daddy!" I called soon as I saw him. He was digging in the dirt with his hands, and beside the hole was four jars of soup from the barn.

He put his hand on one knee and began to push himself up. "Hallelujah!"

"Don't stop!" I said. "Mrs. Cobb is on her way!"

I ran past the woodpile, past the clothesline where Mama's quilt still hung on the line. I ran past Delilah, who started braying soon as she saw me.

I grinned. Good old Delilah. I'd give her ears a good long scratch just as soon as I saw Mama.

The cabin looked like a mansion to me. Better than Mrs. Cobb's house, better than anything I saw in Camden. I took the steps two at a time and pushed open the door.

It was the smell that hit me first. The shutters was closed so I couldn't see too good, and the stench nearly knocked me over. It was worse than the outhouse on a steamy August day. I covered my nose and mouth with one hand and held on to the lunch sack with the other. Had to swallow hard to keep from gagging.

"Mama?" I lifted my head and breathed through my mouth.

No answer.

I took two steps toward the bed. She was buried under a pile of quilts, so I couldn't see her face.

"Mama? It's Ludelphia."

"Lu?" she said, her voice raw as she shifted in the bed.

I forgot about the smell as I moved the quilts away from her face.

Oh, Mama!

Her eyes wasn't stuck together no more, but they was red and swollen. And her hair was matted in places, like it ain't been cleaned good. She looked worse than I had ever seen her. But she was talking, and she knew who I was.

When I touched my fingers to her blistered lips, she let out an awful moan. I backed away from her without even knowing it. The sounds she was making wasn't people sounds, they was the sounds of a dying animal.

"I brought you some medicine, Mama." I held out the lunch sack like a basket of berries and began to pull the bottles out. "Went all the way across the river to fetch it for you."

The second bottle was slippery in my fingers. I fumbled around till the quilt top fell to the floor. When I bent to pick it up my head got to swirling. I reckon on account of the awful smell and finally seeing Mama again after all that running. Plus I ain't even had a bite of that biscuit and ham Mrs. Nelson packed for me.

My knees began to wobble, and the weight of my head seemed to pull me down.

I was falling. Falling so slowly I felt every inch of air as I passed through it. So slowly it was like being inside a dream.

My elbows hit first. Then the bottles. Glass shattered everywhere, spraying clear liquid across the floor and onto Mama. Little pieces of glass dug into my skin, and I could feel blood coming out of the tiny cuts.

The morphine Mrs. Nelson had been so kind to give me found the cracks in the floorboards and folds of the quilt and disappeared.

"No!" I cried. "No!" The medicine in them bottles was my last hope. And now it was gone, all gone.

It was like my muscles was locked up. I couldn't move from the spot on the cabin floor where I was sprawled out. I lay there with my head buried in my arms wishing I could cry. But it was like my eyes was locked up too. The tears wouldn't come.

Wasn't no way around it. I had failed. Mrs. Cobb might as well have shot me instead of that armadillo, for all the good I'd done.

Dear Lord. Mama always said every quilt tells a story. But I didn't want this story. This was not the one I picked out.

"Ludelphia? You okay?" It was Etta Mae. I hadn't even heard her come in.

I wanted to tell her about the medicine, but my tongue felt thick in my mouth. Whatever words I'd thought of before was trapped inside with all them tears.

I stayed on the floor. Mama was still moaning, and there was shouts coming from outside.

Without a sound, Ruben stepped into the cabin. "Mrs. Cobb's pulling up to the Pettways! And she's swinging around a shotgun."

Dear Lord, the shotgun!

As I got my feet up under me, Mrs. Pettway started screaming from out in the yard. "I don't care who you are, you ain't taking this chicken. Mr. Cobb would've never done us this way! You ain't got no right to take this chicken."

"I got every right, Mrs. Pettway." Mrs. Cobb's voice sounded like it was coming from between clenched teeth.

"You gonna have to kill me first. You hear, Mrs. Cobb? You can kill me, but you ain't getting my chicken!"

Ruben looked back at us, his face as worried as mine.

I'd seen what Mrs. Cobb could be like when she got mad. And I wasn't sure if what Mrs. Pettway was doing was brave or just plain dumb.

Then Ruben slipped back toward the door. "You two stay in here with Mama," he said. "Don't you move from this cabin."

Soon as Etta Mae and me both nodded, Ruben let the door close behind him. I didn't have no idea what he was planning to do.

Screams kept coming from outside, and the chickens scrambled beneath the floorboards of the cabin. As the hens squawked and clucked, bits of cotton and chicken feathers flew up through the slats and landed on my skin. The pieces stuck to the bloody places on my hands and arms.

I held my arms out in front of me. I looked like something out of a nightmare. Like a ghost or something from one of Aunt Doshie's visions. Not like a girl at all.

"Etta Mae?" I reached between the slats for more cotton and pressed it against my skin. "Etta Mae, come close!" My head was clear now and my tongue was fine. "I need you."

As Etta Mae got to me, she sucked in her breath. "Mercy, Ludelphia! Gonna take some scrubbing to get you all cleaned up."

No, that wasn't what I was talking about. "First we got to get dirty," I said and wiped my bloody hands across Etta Mae's cheeks.

"What you doing that for?" she said, her eyes wide with alarm. Then she started to back away from me.

"It's the only way, Etta Mae." I reached out again and wiped my hands down the front of her dress. When I got to the torn hem, I gave it a firm yank. The cloth split just like I knew it would. "Don't you see? Mrs. Cobb thinks you and me is witches. So we gonna *be* witches."

As a piece of her dress fluttered to the floor, Etta Mae didn't say a single word. Just stood there letting me do what I was gonna do. I wiped my hands on Etta Mae's dress over and over, till it was so streaked in blood and bits of cotton and tiny feathers that it looked like she'd been rolling around with the chickens under the house. "Now you do me," I said.

Etta Mae squeezed her eyes shut and pressed her hands into the broken glass. She scrunched up her face but she didn't cry out. And when she brought her hands back up her palms was all bloody just like mine.

It was like we had switched places. Now I was the one taking care of Etta Mae. And just like I said to, she wiped her blood on my cheeks and my arms and my dress. We each reached through the floorboards and grabbed up as much cotton as we could get our fingers around. Handful after handful we pressed into our skin till we didn't look nothing like ourselves no more.

Outside the screaming had turned to crying. Mrs. Pettway was wailing like the train I'd heard in Camden. That sound sent chills right through me.

"I'll be back for that chicken," Mrs. Cobb said. "But first I'm going to deal with your neighbors here. The Bennetts."

Dear Lord, Mrs. Cobb was right in front of the cabin!

"Just do what I do," I said, grabbing Etta Mae's hand. "You ain't a witch, and I ain't neither. But if this is the end of Mama's life, I won't have the last thing she sees be Mrs. Cobb taking away everything we got."

Etta Mae squeezed my hand. "Ludelphia Bennett, as I live and breathe, that lady ain't coming into this cabin."

Her eyes glowed as they looked into mine, and I knew whatever happened, we was in it together.

WE CROUCHED INSIDE THE CABIN AND LISTENED to what was happening outside. We was waiting for just the right time to make our move.

"See here, Mr. Bennett," Mrs. Cobb said. "Ain't nothing you got that don't belong to me now."

"But my wife, she's real sick, Mrs. Cobb. If you take that ax, won't be no way for me to chop wood for keeping her warm. And we got a new baby too, just three days old."

"Rose!" I said aloud. I'd forgotten about Rose.

Etta Mae patted my arm. "She's fine, don't you worry. Mrs. Irvin's been looking after her."

I took in a deep breath and let it out real slow. Just as soon as this was all over, I was gonna see Rose for myself. I was gonna hold her in my arms and rock her back and forth.

Outside Daddy went on talking. "Please, Mrs. Cobb! Me and my boy here, we'll work extra hard. I promise we'll make it up to you next planting season. Just give us some time, Mrs. Cobb. All we need is time."

Daddy's words seemed to echo in the silence that followed. For just a moment there was no screaming or snorting, no sound at all. My mind went back to that poor armadillo in Mrs. Cobb's barn. *Hold on, Patrick.* Then *boom!*

Was it the right time yet? My insides was so knotted up, I wasn't sure. So we kept waiting.

When Mrs. Cobb spoke again, her voice was all business. "Gentlemen," she said, "get the animals first. You get me every single one of them chickens and put 'em in that sack with the others. Get the tools too. The ax, the shovel, the pitchfork. And whatever feed you can find in the barn."

"Please, Mrs. Cobb." I knew it was my daddy, but I ain't never heard him beg before. It didn't sound nothing like him.

"And don't forget that mule," Mrs. Cobb went on. "You listening, gentlemen? I want that mule."

I squeezed Etta Mae's hand and pulled her toward the door. *Now* was the time. Wasn't no way Mrs. Cobb was taking Delilah!

Just before we stepped through the doorway, I remembered the knife Mama kept lodged in the wall. The one Etta Mae had put under Mama's mattress and used to cut Rose's cord. I yanked it out of the pine log, then together me and Etta Mae pushed open the door.

"Basheeka basheeba balloo!" I moaned as I walked onto the porch. I waved the knife in circles above my head, careful not to bump Etta Mae. "Basheeka basheeba balloo!" I said it louder. "Basheeka basheeba balloo!" we hollered together as we shook and spun our bodies. The knife danced in the air above us.

From the spot where she was standing next to the corner of the barn, Delilah started to bray. I knew just as long as she could see me, she wasn't gonna stop.

Mrs. Cobb dropped her ledger and looked at me and Etta Mae. She held tight to her shotgun and pressed her other hand against her ear. "What in the world?"

I stabbed the air with the knife, and spit shot out of my mouth. "We're the witches of Gee's Bend! Pass through this doorway and you will *die*!"

Mrs. Cobb took three steps back as Delilah kept up her braying.

"You!" she shouted, pointing a finger at me. "I knew you was a witch!" I waved my arms in the air and moaned like I was possessed by the devil.

"And you!" she hollered at Etta Mae. Mrs. Cobb's eyes widened and she stumbled just a bit.

I wanted her gone, so I grabbed the knife handle with both hands and started shaking my body the way it shook when I rode in that motorcar.

So help me, Lord, she was *not* coming inside this cabin.

Etta Mae glanced at me sideways, then started up with a throaty noise that sounded like something from the deep dark woods that you couldn't see but knew you should run from.

Ruben shot a look my way and I real quick thumped my eye patch same way he always did. His eyes widened and he nudged Daddy in the ribs with his elbow. That's when I knew he understood what we was up to.

"Please, Mrs. Cobb!" Ruben said over Delilah's braying. "My mama's in there dying all because of them witches." Ruben looked over at Daddy, who kept his eyes to the ground. "Don't want something bad to happen to you too!"

Mrs. Cobb pressed her hand harder against the ear as Delilah brayed over and over. "Somebody shut that mule up!"

At first nobody moved. It was like they was all frozen

by Delilah's racket and the sight of me and Etta Mae moaning and shaking and spinning like wild tornadoes.

It was Ruben that broke the spell. "I can take care of that mule for you, Mrs. Cobb. But first you got to give me the gun."

Mrs. Cobb's eyes went all dark. Then, just like in my dream, she lifted the shotgun and aimed.

I closed my eyes. I heard the shot and waited for it to knock me down.

Swing Low, Sweet Chariot

"LUDELPHIA!" ETTA MAE'S VOICE FILLED MY EAR. "Ludelphia, she's leaving! Mrs. Cobb's leaving!" I opened my eye. I looked down at my body. I lifted my feet one at a time.

I was whole. She hadn't shot me at all.

When I looked up, the men had already mounted and was heading on down the road. Mrs. Cobb walked toward the wagon, her shoulders slumped forward. The shotgun dragged behind her, leaving a trail in the dirt.

Was she crying? Was Mrs. Cobb crying? She looked so beaten down, I almost wanted to run over and tell her everything would be okay. I was all mixed up inside because I knew Mrs. Cobb had lost things too. Wasn't no excuse for what she'd done, but I couldn't help remembering that picture on her wall.

Mrs. Cobb slapped the reins and the wagon began to

roll away. The men followed behind her, and soon as they was all past the chinaberry tree, I jumped off the porch to where Daddy was standing at the bottom of the steps.

"I'm sorry, Lu," Daddy said, holding me in his arms.

I wrapped my arms tight as I could around his waist. It was me who should be sorry, not Daddy.

He stroked my braids. "Ain't never seen a mule so disagreeable."

Delilah. She wasn't braying no more.

I pulled away from Daddy so I could get a look at her. That's when I knew what Daddy was sorry about.

Delilah was lying flat out on the ground, and Ruben was on his knees beside her. She wasn't making a single sound, and she wasn't moving neither.

"Delilah," I cried, running toward her. I knelt next to Ruben and I could see there was a hole right through the center of her neck.

Oh, Delilah! Why on earth did you have to go and make all that racket? Why couldn't you ever just keep quiet?

Tears wet my cheeks. What was wrong with Mrs. Cobb that she had to up and kill critters when they was just doing what comes naturally to 'em? Wasn't no reason for her to shoot Delilah. No reason at all.

When Ruben threw his arm around my shoulder, my

whole body began to shake with crying. For as long as I could remember, Delilah had been there waiting for me every morning by the barn. She was always there no matter what.

"It's all my fault," I said, burying my face into Ruben's shoulder.

"Lu," Ruben said, pulling back to look me in the eye, "you just saved the cabin!" He pressed my head to his chest. "We still got our pots and our quilts and our butcher knife. It's gonna be okay, Lu. Everything's gonna be okay."

"But I couldn't save Delilah." Tears kept coming down my cheeks and nose. "And I can't save Mama."

"Only God can do that, Lu," Daddy said. He wrapped his arms around me and Ruben, and he squeezed so hard I thought my ribs would break. "Only God, you hear?"

When I looked up at his face, his eyes was shining. He stroked my cheeks with his big thumbs, tender, like I was a little child. "I won't have you blaming yourself, Lu."

Daddy held my face like that till I nodded. "Now, you and Etta Mae go get cleaned up while me and Ruben take care of Delilah. Can't have your mama seeing you like this."

Soon as Daddy let me loose, I turned back to Delilah. I gave her one last stroke between the eyes. That's when

I knew it could've been me lying there on the ground. If Delilah hadn't been braying like crazy and if Mrs. Cobb hadn't swung her shotgun, it could've been me. In a way Delilah had saved my life.

I wanted to go in the cabin right that minute and tell Mama there was some things that no matter how fine the cloth, no matter how straight the stitches, there was some things that was never gonna go in a quilt. Like how loud the quiet was now that I knew Delilah was never gonna bray again. Some stories you just got to hold in your heart.

I looked around the yard for the bucket, but it wasn't noplace in sight. I reckon it was in the back of Mrs. Cobb's wagon.

Me and Etta Mae walked down to the spring together, but we didn't say nothing till we was there. So much had happened it was hard to know what to say first.

Etta Mae pulled her dress over her head and set it on the ground. "Soon as Aunt Doshie told us what Willie Joe said about the ferry busting loose, I knew you was in trouble, Lu." Etta Mae smiled. "Me and Ruben went all up and down the river looking for you. Even had to spend the night in the woods. Wasn't till this morning that we decided to check Camden."

I picked at the bits of cotton and feathers on my arms.

Wasn't nothing more Etta Mae and Ruben could have done. "If you'd come too soon, then I might not have gotten to taste a genuine Coca-Cola."

"A Coke? Did it fizz all the way down your throat?"

"That's right." I grinned. "Sure do wish you could have been there to play Mrs. Cobb's piano. It was so big it nearly took up the whole room."

Etta Mae splashed water onto her arms. "Was it maple, like the one I played in Mobile?"

"No, black. The shiniest most beautiful black you ever did see."

"Listen to you," she said, a grin coming across her face. "You done been out in the world, Ludelphia. All on your own." The smile disappeared. "You don't need me no more. Not like you used to."

"Sure I do," I said, my teeth chattering. "Ain't nobody else in Gee's Bend that can suck the poison out of a bee sting good as you."

Etta Mae smiled, then her face got all serious. "Lu, you know I loved that baby, Sarah, more than anything. Broke my heart when she died."

I grabbed her hand. "I know, Etta Mae. The doctor's wife told me what happened. She said it wasn't no fault of yours."

Etta Mae's fingers squeezed mine. "Wasn't your fault about Mrs. Cobb neither. You hear me, Lu?"

I knew what she was saying was true. But tears came into my eyes again anyhow. In just three days, my whole life had changed. Wasn't nothing I needed that wasn't right here in Gee's Bend. And wasn't a thing that could happen that I wasn't strong enough to get through.

"Mercy, it's cold," Etta Mae said, rubbing the goose bumps first from my arms, then from hers. "Reckon we best get on back."

Real quick we dunked our dresses till the water ran clear. Once we was dressed again, I grabbed a handful of that bloody cotton. It would dry out, and nobody but me would ever know about it. But when it came time to set my quilt top up in the frame, I was gonna stuff them bits right between the seams. So I wouldn't never forget that part of my story.

Etta Mae went to her cabin, and I went to mine. Ruben met me just inside the door where he was sweeping the glass pieces off the floor. The room still smelled sour, but somebody had thrown open the window shutter, so it didn't seem bad as before.

"What about Delilah?" I said as I walked across to where Daddy was sitting on the edge of Mama's bed.

"Wish we could've buried her, but ain't a shovel left in Gee's Bend," Daddy said. "So we dragged her up near the swamp."

I swallowed back tears. Poor Delilah. Just wasn't fair what happened to her.

Daddy patted the bed beside him as Mama slept. "I know it's hard," he said. "But I reckon the old girl's in a better place now. Don't know what we would have fed her nohow. Mrs. Cobb done took every scrap of corn and grain in that barn. Gonna be hard enough feeding ourselves."

"What about Mama?" I wrapped a quilt around my wet shoulders and sat next to Daddy.

"Lu, you was the one that went to see the doctor. What did he say?"

I hung my head. Might as well go on and tell him. "Doc Nelson said wasn't nothing to be done." I remembered the little brown bottles. "He said wasn't no medicine yet for pneumonia. And that morphine Mrs. Nelson gave me . . . ain't a drop of it left."

Daddy sighed and rubbed his eyes. Then he put his hand on my knee. "We just got to keep on doing what we been doing. I ain't seen no more blood since you left. She ain't no better, but I don't reckon she's no worse neither."

Ruben stopped his sweeping and leaned against the broom. "Seems like she's breathing easier since you got back, Lu. I think she knew you was gone before."

I leaned over so I could get a good look at Mama. Was it possible? Was it really possible that Mama might make it? That she might hold and nurse her new baby girl?

"Daddy," I said, "I want Rose back. Now that I'm here, ain't no reason for her to be up at the Irvins'. She belongs here. With her family."

Daddy pressed his lips together and nodded. "Don't reckon you need me to tell you it's all right to go get her. Not when you big enough to go all the way to Camden on your own."

My heart started beating real fast. Was Daddy mad at me? With everything else that had happened, I sure couldn't take him being mad at me.

"Daddy," I said, my voice shaking.

He grinned then. Wasn't a big grin, but I knew what it meant. "I'm just glad you made it home safe and sound, Lu. That's all that matters."

I threw my arms around him and buried my face in his neck. "Thank you, Daddy." His skin was sticky with sweat and he smelled of dirt. I don't reckon there's a smell in the world better than that.

"Go on, then," he said after a minute. "Best go before

it gets dark. I'll sit here with your mama while you and Ruben go fetch Rose."

I turned to give Mama one last look. "Be right back, Mama. I won't be gone so long this time. And when I come back, I'm gonna bring you your baby girl." Mama didn't say a word, just lay there sleeping.

"You want these?" Ruben said as I walked away from the bed. He held my quilt top, the soggy paper sack and a scrap of yellow cloth in his hands.

I looked him in the eye. "Thank you, Ruben. Not just for this, but for coming after me."

"When you didn't make it home for supper, I knew wasn't no choice but for me and Etta Mae to go find you."

I rolled down the top of the bag. "It wasn't anything like I thought it'd be."

Ruben thumped my eye patch. "Now you know."

The evening air was cool as me and Ruben set out on the footpath to Pleasant Grove Baptist Church. As we walked past the Pettways, I saw Etta Mae sitting with her mama and daddy on the front porch.

"Ain't got nothing left," Mrs. Pettway said as she rocked herself back and forth. And I reckon it was true. Even that chicken Mrs. Pettway had held so tight to was gone. Wasn't no animal sounds coming from under the cabin or in the barn.

"Well, we got them hogs up there in the woods," Mr. Pettway said. "They'll come back when it's feeding time."

"But we ain't got no knife to butcher 'em with or a skillet or a single potato." Mrs. Pettway's voice was more like a whine. "And it's getting colder by the day. How are we gonna live? You tell me that. How are we gonna eat and keep ourselves warm?"

"Shhh, Mama," Etta Mae said. "Shhh."

But it didn't do no good. Mrs. Pettway kept right on rocking and crying. And I reckon she had every reason to carry on. Wasn't nothing none of us could say that would change the way things was. So me and Ruben just kept on walking.

Sure enough, the windows of Pleasant Grove Baptist Church was lit with candles and inside we could see the place was packed full of folks. And it wasn't even a Sunday.

Inside the room was too loud to talk, and it made me think of all them ladies at the Red Cross drive. Folks was crying, and over and over again I heard the words "Mrs. Cobb." It was like a hurricane had blown through and now everybody had to talk about every little thing that happened. Where they was. What was said. What they lost.

Aunt Doshie was there, sitting in her usual spot. For once she wasn't saying a single thing to anybody. Just sitting there listening.

As we made our way toward the front of the church where Mrs. Irvin always sat, Reverend Irvin stood to address the crowd. "Children of the Lord," he began, his tall, thin body swaying.

"Mrs. Irvin," I said as folks quieted and began to take their seats, "thank you for helping with the baby."

Ruben smiled at her. "Don't know what we would have done without you."

She pulled the quilt away from Rose's face. "Your mama's doing better, then?"

I sucked in my breath and didn't hear a word of Ruben's answer to the question.

"Rose!" I said. "Baby Rose!" Her eyes was closed and I could see her tiny black eyelashes. I reached out my arms and next thing I knew, Rose's warm body was right up next to my heart. Her cheeks looked fuller to me, her face more round. She was already growing.

I stroked Rose's hair. "Can you believe it, Ruben?"

"Let's get her home," Ruben said. "So she can be with her mama."

Mrs. Irvin's lap looked empty. "Keep her bundled up," she said, clasping her hands like she didn't know what to do with 'em. "Babies sleep best when they're nice and warm."

As Mrs. Irvin turned her attention to Reverend Irvin, me and Ruben made our way to the back of the church and out the door.

The voices from inside the church followed us back down the footpath. First it was just Reverend Irvin all by himself. Then it was everybody together.

"Swing low, sweet chariot," they sang, "coming for to carry me home. Swing low, sweet chariot, coming for to carry me home."

Me and Ruben's eyes met, then we was singing too. "I looked over Jordan, and what did I see, coming for to carry me home? A band of angels coming after me, coming for to carry me home."

All the way home we sang for all that had been lost that day, and for all that had been saved. Wasn't no better words than the ones in that song.

Back at the cabin, Ruben held open the door for me as I carried Rose straight to the bed and placed her next to Mama.

"Look at that," Daddy said. I knew just what he was talking about. Mama and Rose fit together snug as puzzle pieces.

I watched 'em for a while, then I watched the flames

stretch and curl as Ruben stoked the fire. Then I picked up my quilting things. It was time for me to start over.

I set right to work pulling the stitches out of the part I'd already done. Then I laid out all the pieces, same as I'd seen Mama do. The calico ones from Mama's apron went in one pile, the rough burlap ones from the pocket of my sack dress in another, the fancy white napkin Mrs. Cobb gave me in another.

From the lunch sack I pulled Doc Nelson's blue handkerchief and the scrap I tore from Etta Mae's dress. The handkerchief I ripped into four skinny strips. The yellow piece from Etta Mae's dress I tore into squares. Then I took off my eye patch. This time for good.

With the needle and spool of thread Mrs. Nelson gave me, I tied a knot and started stitching. It was gonna take a while to finish, but I wanted to get the most important part done right away.

I dusted off the little triangle of denim that had been my eye patch and took off the string. Then I set one of the calico pieces next to it and pushed my needle in and out. Now that I was back home in the cabin with my whole family beside me, wasn't nothing to stop me from telling my story just the way it happened.

Winter

THE WEEKS THAT CAME AFTER MRS. COBB LOADED up her wagons was the coldest anybody could remember. Wasn't just cold, it was quiet. It was like a thick fog had settled over all of Gee's Bend. Only wasn't no sun to chase it away.

The worst part was not having nothing to eat except hackberries and wild plums. We was so proud when Mrs. Cobb didn't take our pots, but what good was they when there wasn't no food to put in 'em?

Didn't take but two days for the four jars of soup Daddy buried in the yard to get gone. I reckon we could have made 'em last longer if we hadn't shared with the Pettways and Aunt Doshie. But Daddy said we was all in this together, and together we would get through it.

One day Daddy made a slingshot out of a hickory branch and some leather pieces he found in the barn.

After that you could find him hunting in the woods most afternoons. Usually he'd come home with his hands in his pockets. So my ears perked right up the day I heard him whistling before I could see him.

"Daddy? Is it a deer?" I said. What I would give for some deer meat! My belly started jumping just at the thought of it.

"Even better," he said, his cheeks glowing. Better than a deer? I couldn't think of nothing that would be better than that. But I reckon anything would be good so long as it wasn't more berries.

"Don't peek," Daddy said. So I closed my eyes and held my breath.

"All right, open 'em," Daddy said.

"A squirrel? You caught a squirrel?" My belly started churning real strong. Squirrel was tough but it was tasty. And a little meat would be good for Mama. Be good for all of us, but especially Mama.

Daddy grinned. "Just look at that fat belly! Gonna be some good eating tonight."

"I'll go put some water on," I said, heading back inside the cabin.

"Mama," I said once the door was shut behind me, "gonna have us some squirrel stew for supper. Won't that be a treat?"

Mama didn't speak but her lips curved into a smile. She was lying up in the bed same as she did every day. Wasn't much else she could do, but at least she wasn't getting them coughing spells near as much as she used to. And seemed like she was staying awake more and more.

"Got to be patient," Aunt Doshie said last time she looked in on Mama. "Gonna take some time for her to get her strength back." Wasn't no more talk about Mama dying or about what I done or about Etta Mae being a witch. It was like Mrs. Cobb took all that mess right out of Aunt Doshie's head along with all them things she hauled out of Gee's Bend.

Wasn't nothing left but important things to talk about. Like how things sure was tough, but we was tougher. Mrs. Cobb might have taken all the things we owned, but we still had each other, and together we was gonna make it.

"Ruben?" Mama said as I stoked the fire.

"Gone fishing." It was what he did most every day now. Sometimes I'd go with him, but I still got tired of all that waiting. And so far Ruben ain't caught a single fish. But he kept on trying.

Things would have been better if we was having school like we usually did during the winter months. But Reverend Irvin said Teacher wasn't coming, on account nobody had nothing to pay him with.

When I first heard about it, I wanted to kick something real hard. Then I started thinking about Patrick and how he had all those children to feed. Could be Teacher had even more children than Patrick. I reckon he wanted to come teach us but needed something more filling than hackberries.

Wasn't nothing to be done about it. Just meant time dragged on slower than it might have if we was spending half the day learning our lessons over at Pleasant Grove Baptist Church.

I kept close to the fire as the flames under the pot crackled. Too bad there wasn't nothing but water to put in with the squirrel. Some potatoes or carrots sure would be good. I reckon this squirrel stew was gonna taste about as exciting as pine bark. Or biscuits with no lard in 'em.

"Ain't got nothing to complain about," I reminded myself. Sometimes it helped to say it out loud. We was blessed to have that squirrel, even if it wasn't much. I reckon it was more than a lot of folks had, and it was important to remember that part.

But there was so many things I missed about the way things used to be before Mrs. Cobb came with her wagons. Like the sound of the hens scratching and clucking. And eggs. I sure did miss cracking eggs for corn bread. I even missed the sound of Mama's broom banging the dirt out of the quilts on the line.

Most of all I missed Delilah. Sometimes the quiet got to me so bad I wanted to scream. But I couldn't do that. Not with Mama needing me to be strong. So I stomped my feet instead. Just so I could hear the floorboards squeak and groan.

From her pallet at the foot of Mama's bed, Rose stirred. Her big brown eyes was open and her brow was all drawn up. She liked looking at all them colors on my quilt top. Rose wasn't no bigger than a hambone, but already she liked quilts.

Wasn't a day that passed that I didn't take up my needle and cloth pieces and put in some stitches. I was right to start over. And I ain't missed my eye patch, not once.

Before long it would be time for me to set it up in the quilting frame. Which is why I paid good attention when the ladies started talking at church. But so far not a one of 'em had said a thing about quilting.

As the water in the pot began to boil, I watched Daddy through the doorway of the cabin. He wiped his knife across his britches and held the squirrel meat in the air.

Then Ruben came running down the footpath. Wasn't a fishing pole or nothing in his hands.

"A wagon's coming!" he hollered. "A white man in a wagon!"

Hadn't been no wagons in Gee's Bend since Mrs. Cobb came. Surely it wasn't one of her men coming back for something. Not after two whole months.

I rushed into the yard, my heart pounding. All the Pettways came pouring out of their cabin, but wasn't no words spoken. We was all just waiting to see who it was.

The wagon didn't stop till it got to the chinaberry tree in our front yard. I squinted my eye. Could it be? Could it really be?

"Doc Nelson!" I cried as I ran toward him. It *was* Doc Nelson! He was finally here to check on my mama!

His face broke into a grin as he stepped out of the wagon. "Ludelphia Bennett," he said, his dimple flashing. Same as it had the very first time I saw him. "Just the person I was coming to see."

I threw my arms around him and held tight. Didn't matter that he wasn't family or that it had been so long. He had come all the way to Gee's Bend, just like I asked him to!

"You here to check on my mama?"

"That's part of it." He stroked his chin. "How's she doing?"

"Better," I said. "Aunt Doshie says it's just gonna take some time."

Doc Nelson nodded his head and breathed deep. Like a load had been lifted from his back. "Glad to hear it, Ludelphia. Right glad to hear it."

Daddy walked up to us and held out his hand.

"Mr. Bennett?" Doc Nelson said, giving his hand a shake. "That's a fine daughter you got there. I know you're proud of her."

"Yessir," Daddy said. "What brings you to Gee's Bend?"

"Two things. I wanted to look in on your wife, and I wanted to bring you this letter." Doc Nelson pulled a piece of paper from his shirt pocket and handed it to Daddy.

Daddy took it from him, then slowly unfolded the paper. "Ain't bad news, is it? Can't take any more bad news."

Ruben and the Pettways all moved in close so they could see better. "Read it to us, Daddy," I said. I wanted to snatch it out of his hand and read it myself, but I forced myself to stand still and listen.

Daddy cleared his throat. "Dear Ludelphia Bennett." He stopped and took a sideways look at me. "Thank you for alerting us to the dire conditions in Gee's Bend,

Alabama. The Red Cross is here to help, so we are sending this shipment to help ease the pain and suffering in your town. Another shipment will follow. Sincerely, The American Red Cross."

Shipment? I looked at Doc Nelson's wagon. Why, it was piled high with boxes. Wasn't no telling what all was in 'em!

"See, Daddy?" I said, rushing to the wagon. "See that red cross?" Each box had a label on it. So there was no mistaking who it was from.

Daddy's eyes got wet, and Ruben let out a whoop. "Can you believe it?" Ruben said to Etta Mae.

Etta Mae started to laugh then till her whole body was shaking. "Sure, I do," she said to Ruben. "Ain't nothing Lu can't do." A look passed between 'em then. A look that made me think of Mama and Daddy when they was together and they thought nobody was watching. Did it mean what I thought it meant?

Wasn't no time for me to think about it. Not with Doc Nelson and his wagon standing right there.

"There's cornmeal and sugar," Doc Nelson said as he walked around the wagon and read off the labels on the boxes. "Meat and dried beans. . . ." He lifted one of the bags to look underneath. "Got some seed and fertilizer too."

Mr. Pettway lifted his hands to the heavens and Mrs. Pettway's eyes filled right up with tears. But she was smiling too. Not like the day Mrs. Cobb came at all.

I wanted to dance, I wanted to sing! I wanted to take Daddy's hand and do the two-step. I touched the bag that was marked flour. It was smooth cotton, the kind a needle goes through easy as rain through the roof.

"Thanks to your daughter, Mr. Bennett, now somebody out there knows there's a Gee's Bend," Mr. Nelson said, giving my shoulder a gentle pat. "Won't be forgotten now. Not after this."

I let the warmth spread through my arms and legs, all the way to my ears and toes. Even though I knew it wasn't really me who'd done it. It was Mrs. Nelson that sent my letter.

When I looked over at Daddy, I could see tears sparkling in his eyelashes. I ran over and wrapped my arms around his waist. I linked my hands and squeezed just as hard as I could.

"Look what you done, Ludelphia." Daddy pumped my hand just like I'd seen him do with Ruben when my brother brought in more cotton than anybody else. Then he wiped his eyes and looked up at the sky. "Hallelujah," he whispered. "Hallelujah!"

THINGS WAS BETTER IN GEE'S BEND AFTER DOC Nelson brought them Red Cross boxes.

The biggest thing was I didn't wake in the middle of the night with my belly rumbling. There was biscuits for breakfast, and bacon too. There was jars of vegetables and corn bread for supper. Wasn't near as good as when Mama was cooking it, but it was solid food.

"Got to be careful we don't eat it too fast," Daddy said. Wasn't no telling how long the cold would last. So we stored some on the shelves in the barn.

But it wasn't just about the food. It was like the air wasn't near as cold as it had been, and folks was smiling more. The ladies at the church even started up quilting again. Didn't take but one Sunday afternoon for all of us working together to get my quilt finished.

Things was better with Mama too. Within two weeks

of Doc Nelson's visit, she was strong enough to get out of bed all on her own and walk across the cabin.

"Don't want you doing too much," Daddy said.

"Stop your worrying," Mama said with a smile. She was wearing a pair of white knit socks that came in one of them Red Cross boxes. I was wearing a pair too. Them socks kept my toes warm and toasty the rest of that winter.

"Mama, you about ready to try out them shoes you picked?" They was from the Red Cross boxes too. The day Doc Nelson came, Daddy carried in a few pairs for Mama to see. She picked some shiny leather ones for herself and some little bitty ones for Rose to have when she started walking. But so far she ain't put them shoes on her feet.

Not like Ruben. Wasn't nobody faster getting on them boots than he was. And he sure did like to bang around in 'em. For days afterwards, he toted the wood and water and put out the wash too, just to feel the weight of them boots on his feet.

"I'm saving mine for church," Mama said. "Soon as I'm well enough to walk to church, that's when I'm gonna put them fancy shoes on." Mama looked at me from across the room. "But that don't have to stop you from wearing yours."

"It ain't that, Mama. It's just I don't like 'em." I'd picked a pair of high-heeled ones with little straps, just like in the picture on the cabin wall. I stomped 'em into the dirt to see the prints they made. But they cramped my little toes and rubbed raw spots into my heels. So wasn't long before I took 'em off again. I reckon after all that happened, I just needed to feel the dirt of Gee's Bend same as I always had, right between my toes.

"Best hold on to 'em," Mama said. "For when you change your mind."

"Yes'm," I said. Even though I couldn't imagine a time coming that I'd ever want to wear them shoes. But one thing I'd learned in the three months since Rose was born was that Mama's right about most everything. All them things she was always telling me? So far every one of 'em had turned out to be true.

"Ludelphia Bennett," Mama said, looking at me hard for the first time in a long time, "where is your eye patch?"

I grinned. I'd been waiting for just this moment. "Right here, Mama," I said as I reached underneath the stack of quilts in the corner where I'd hidden the one I made for her.

When I held it up and pointed to the little triangle of

denim, Mama lifted her eyebrows and her eyes got wide. "You done this, Ludelphia? All by yourself?"

I nodded. Then Mama took it from my hands and ran her fingers along the seams. "Must be some story," she said as she touched the pieces that came from her apron, then the ones that used to be the blue handkerchief and finally the bright yellow ones I'd set in each corner.

"Tell me," she said, swinging the quilt up and around her shoulders just like I imagined she would. "From start to finish."

And so I did. But first I asked her the question I'd been aching to ask all this time. "Mama?" I said. "Did you really believe it when Aunt Doshie told you Etta Mae was a witch?"

Mama fingered the eye patch on the quilt. "It's ain't as simple as believing or not believing." My heart sank down to the pit of my stomach. It wasn't the answer I wanted. "Lu, I got to tell you, sometimes things don't make sense, no matter how hard you try to figure it. Sometimes none of the rules fit." I looked her in the eye. Now we was getting someplace! "Them are the times you got to find the courage to do what you think is best. You got to make up your own mind and see it through."

I grinned. "Just like stitching a quilt."

"That's right," Mama said. "Now tell me everything."

Once I started telling it, there wasn't no stopping me. Wasn't a single thing I left out. And by the time I got to the part about Mrs. Cobb giving me a Coke to drink, Ruben and Daddy was listening too.

Even Rose was listening. And when I held up the quilt to show my story piece by piece, that baby girl squealed and gurgled like she was gonna start talking right then and there. I mean to tell you, there ain't nothing sweeter in this whole wide world.

Things was different between me and Mama after that. She didn't worry after me the way she used to. And I didn't wear no eye patch ever again.

I don't reckon I have to tell you Mama sure was right about them shoes. I changed my mind all right.

But that's a different quilt. And a whole other story.

Author's Note

LEAVING GEE'S BEND is a fictional story that evolved out of my love for quilts and other textile arts. The daughter of a seamstress, I grew up watching my mother use a needle and sewing machine to create works of art out of plain pieces of fabric. So when I learned The Quilts of Gee's Bend art exhibit would be on display at the Whitney Museum of American Art during a trip to New York City, I knew I needed to see it. (Yes, even though Gee's Bend is located only 120 miles from my home in Birmingham, Alabama, I had to travel all the way to New York City to view the exhibit!)

Something happened to me as I walked through those rooms. I was moved by the colors and textures, and by the voices of the quiltmakers as they told their stories. For weeks afterward, their words woke me in the mornings and sang me to sleep at night. I wanted to know anything and everything about this place and its people, so I began to feed my obsession by reading whatever I could find about Gee's Bend. And I began to write about what I was feeling, first in a poem entitled "The Quilts of Gee's Bend," which appeared in *Whatever Remembers Us: An Anthology of Alabama Poetry* (Negative Capability Press, 2007), and later in prose. I completed three novels set in Gee's Bend before I found within myself the story I meant to tell all along: Ludelphia's story, *Leaving Gee's Bend*.

There are many fascinating events in the history of Gee's Bend, but it was the photographs Arthur Rothstein took for the Resettlement Administration in 1937 that most captivated me. Then when I read firsthand accounts of the 1932 raid on Gee's Bend and later learned of the subsequent Red Cross rescue, I knew this was the experience I most wanted to write about. The people who lived through this terrible time possess a strength and faith I admire and want only to honor. To that end, I chose to name my characters using surnames that are common in Gee's Bend even now: Bennett and Pettway. The characters in this book are completely fictional, but they are certainly inspired by the stories told by the actual residents of Gee's Bend.

If you would like to know more about these real people and this place called Gee's Bend, please see the beautiful book *Gee's Bend: The Women and Their Quilts* and its companion, *The Quilts of Gee's Bend: Masterpieces from a Lost Place* (Tinwood Books, 2002). There is also a film entitled *The Quiltmakers of Gee's Bend* that was produced by Alabama Public Television in association with Hunter Films in 2005. Also, there is not a finer piece of writing than the 2000 Pulitzer Prize–winning article by J. R. Moehringer, "Crossing Over," that chronicles the story of Mary Lee Bendolph and her relationship with the Alabama River. There is also an incredible stage play by Elyzabeth Gregory Wilder called *Gee's Bend*.

Currently Gee's Bend is officially known as Boykin, Alabama. Its quilting tradition continues to thrive even as the population dwindles. The ferry runs daily between Camden and Gee's Bend, and at the time of this writing is operated by Hornblower Marine Services.

Acknowledgments

It takes an army to write a book, and this one was blessed with many wonderful warriors. I thank you all and ask your forgiveness for the names I am bound to leave out.

First and foremost, I'd like to thank the quilters of Gee's Bend for each and every stitch that goes into the making of a quilt. Thanks also to Bill Arnett for bringing these amazing works of art into museums across the country. And to all the teachers, librarians, writers, historians and photographers who have made it their business to document and share the history of Gee's Bend, I thank you for making the research part of writing this book a real joy. Any errors are mine alone.

Special thanks to my agent Rosemary Stimola for her steadfast guidance. Thanks also to the crew at Putnam, most especially my gifted editor Stacey Barney, who took a chance on a skeleton of a story and made just the right observations and asked just the right questions to help me grow a full-fledged novel. And to all the Tenners: I can't imagine a better group of writers with whom to share the journey.

Thanks to the following people who read early drafts of this and/or other stories: Amy Badham, Lynn Baker, Jerri Beck, Lori Ditoro, Evelyn Dykes, Jennifer M. Dykes, Ken Dykes, Sr., Pam Freeman, Cayley Griffiths, Sarah Griffiths, Mary Hughs, Roger Hughs, Allen Johnson, Bobbie Latham, Paul Latham, Russ Nelson, Carol Norton, Jim Reed, Mary Ann Rodman, Debbie Parvin, Stephanie Shaw, Seth Tanner, Pam Toler, Debbie Whalen, Jan Young.

Thanks also to Granddaddy, Grandma, Mama, Papa, Stan, Ken II, Lynn and MicaJon for giving me such colorful cloth to work with. And to Paul, Daniel, Andrew and Eric: you are the needle and thread in my pocket. Thank you.